Nicodemus

A Fluke Journey

RANDY L MARSING

BALBOA.PRESS
A DIVISION OF HAY HOUSE

Balboa Press books may be ordered through booksellers or by contacting:

Balboa Press
A Division of Hay House
1663 Liberty Drive
Bloomington, IN 47403
www.balboapress.com
844-682-1282

Because of the dynamic nature of the Internet, any web addresses or links contained in this book may have changed since publication and may no longer be valid. The views expressed in this work are solely those of the author and do not necessarily reflect the views of the publisher, and the publisher hereby disclaims any responsibility for them.

The author of this book does not dispense medical advice or prescribe the use of any technique as a form of treatment for physical, emotional, or medical problems without the advice of a physician, either directly or indirectly. The intent of the author is only to offer information of a general nature to help you in your quest for emotional and spiritual well-being. In the event you use any of the information in this book for yourself, which is your constitutional right, the author and the publisher assume no responsibility for your actions.

Any people depicted in stock imagery provided by Getty Images are models, and such images are being used for illustrative purposes only. Certain stock imagery © Getty Images.

Print information available on the last page.

ISBN: 979-8-7652-3921-6 (sc)
ISBN: 979-8-7652-3922-3 (e)

Balboa Press rev. date: 02/15/2023

Contents

Chapter 1

I was walking through the forest one dark, starry night. I could hear the leaves rustle in the breeze as it whistled a low and lonely tune through the boughs of the trees. Looking up I caught a glimpse of a shooting star, following it I saw a single cloud and the moon, I thought I could see a smile on the moon's face. As I reached the depths of the woodlands solitude I stood still. I began to hear the creatures come to life, each with its own melody. The crickets, owls and the frogs upon the pond. The pond sparkled like the sky full of twinkling stars. Soon the melody was an acoustic blend of life unseen. Carefully I walked to the edge of the water so as not to disturb the peacefulness of the moment. As I stared at the iridescent moon upon the water, I caught a glance of something aglow beyond the shore. Did it move? Was it a reflection? I found myself scanning the vastness before me. There! No, well maybe. Yes! Certainly there, among the reeds near the willows. A firefly? I have never seen one before, yet I have heard of such a thing and that it really exists. Where has it gone? I look, mesmerized, fixed into the darkness and yet It is all I see.

The peacefulness is overwhelming. I am content and at ease, still I think of how nice it would be to share such a wonderful experience with someone dear to me, but who? I am alone. My mind began to drift away in thought my eyes flickered. Suddenly I heard a splash upon the water. Again I became aware of my surroundings. I noticed the ripples moving from side to side. Startled, I look around, the sound of the night creatures still in rhythm and undisturbed. Again the splash,

I turn my head to see the ripples working their way toward the shore. I began to concentrate on the center of the ripples, surveying the surrounding area with my peripheral vision. There! Brightly colored, beneath the moonlight, a fish brilliant with red and aqua scales. It leaped into the reeds and a flash of light began to head toward me. The rainbow colored fish leaped frantically in its quest to devour the light. To my amazement I ducked as the light zipped past me. Looking up, it is gone and the pond begins to calm once again. Sitting up startled by what had just happened my mind searches for answers as my eyes scan eagerly for the light. Did I hear something as the light headed for me? I'm not sure but I am curious. As I gave thought to the moment I believed I heard what seemed to be a whisper, yet turning I saw nothing. My mind wonders, searching for a logical explanation. The wind has ceased yet the creatures of the night sing on.

Overwhelmed with the idea of, "What if", I began to call out, "Hello, is anyone there? I am friendly, I wish you no harm." To my great amazement I was answered, I heard a small voice say Hello". The sound is highly pitched and feminine, my body responds with goose bumps. There is hesitation in my thoughts and I am without words. I look for a visual answer and see none. Again I hear a soft, "Hello", "Hello to you." I turned my head and beheld the light right before me. I wiped my eyes, rubbing them, then opened them slowly. My vision clears to a light before them and again I hear the voice clear and sweet. "What are you?" Dumbfounded, my response is, "Excuse me, did you say something?" I felt odd as the words left my mouth, and astonished at my response to this unknown interaction; although, all I can see is a light, the words are quite clear. "Hello, what are you?" "I am Nicodemus! Who, and what are you?" I asked. The words flow into my ears, I am Tila and I am here before you. I am the light you see, but to see me as I truly am you must find and eat the special plant that will open your mind and eyes." I said, "How will I find this plant?' I am eager, and curious. "I shall show you, follow me." Leaving the place by the lake's shore I began to follow the light before me.

Quickly we traveled past the trees where the ground was overgrown with flowers the colors of which I have never seen before.

I also noticed the abundance of that which surrounded me was of such visual awe I lost sight of the light and became concerned. As I looked around seeking the light, I heard the soft voice, "Over here." I lifted my head and as if in a sacred place. I see before me a waterfall. The bluest of blues and clear as crystal. To the side the ferns grow, overlapping the cliff which I had fallen into. "Here". There below the light, a yellow berry, shaped like a pear hanging from a short vine with large dark green leaves outlined with a yellow trim. "Eat!' The words were clear. I am hesitant. "You will be able to see me clearly if you eat one of these berries." Now I am eager to see what I cannot. I reach to pick a berry and the light speeds away. Simultaneously, we say, "Do not be afraid." As I put the berry in my mouth the plant disappeared, the berry began to melt coating my tongue. My eyes became blurry and I had to sit to keep from falling, for I seemed to have lost my balance. I closed my eyes and shook my head. I opened my eyes. There, sitting on a bright orange mushroom, was a beautiful creature, with pearl-essence wings glistening like fire opals. She had long curly gold hair and rosy red cheeks. She was shapely, like a woman considered attractive and appealing. There were two small antennae on top of her head peeking out from the golden curls. Again she said, my name is Tila, what are you? I asked, "What am I Oh! I am a young man. A Man she said Yes, a man, a human. I said. Then she said, "I have heard of such creatures but I have never encountered one before. Are you a fairy I asked I have heard tales of fairies but I have never seen one, nor did I believe in them until now That is what you are, is it not? She replied yes, we are guardians of the sacred forest." I questioned, "How come you speak my language so well?" She replied, "it is not that I speak your language, it is only that we can now understand each other. As you can see me, so can you speak to me and understand me. Where do you come from?" Answering her I said, I come from beyond the forest, there is a village where there are many more like me." She wondered and asked, "Are they as nice as you?" I replied. "There are many different kinds of humans, or people, some are nice and some are very mean." "OH!", she exclaimed, "People like that must never know we exist, that is why you had to eat the berry so we could communicate verbally and visually." Why did you choose me? I wondered and she answered without my asking. "I could hear your thoughts by the sacred pond. Your heart is kind and you were feeling lonely." I explained to her how I was shocked and yet grateful that she had made herself known to me. I was lonely even with all those people around me, my heart was empty and I wanted to find some peace in what was an otherwise hectic life. That was how I had come to know of the forest. I had wandered in a time or two but never as far as I had on this occasion. Tila explained that she had seen me before and was curious as to my being. I thanked her and she said she was pleased we could interact. I told her that she could call me Nicky.

Our conversation continued. "You said you have heard of fairies before, what is that you heard?" I explained that fairy tales are quite popular and there are movies with fairies in them, which bring a magical wonder to the story. Tila asked me how anyone would know about fairies. I didn't have an answer.

As I looked around I noticed that my surroundings were changing. Almost everything had a fluorescent glow about it, sparkling and colorful. I noticed other creatures skurring about, busy, they reminded me of people busily going to work or out to play. I asked Tila if there were other fairies. She explained that there were. She said there were other woodland inhabitants that were not fairies they too were alive and able to communicate. She explained the sacredness of the woodland and said that violation would terminate the ability to communicate in all forms. "Nicky, there are things I can show you that are very special and beautiful in our world. There are many things I would like to know about your world and its wonders." We sat there under the stars and sooner that I had wishes they began to fade as dawn approached. I explained to Tila that I had to leave and that I would return. Sadly she asked when I thought I might come back… I told her I would come back tomorrow, at the same time in the evening at the pond. We said our good-byes and she flew away. I left the forest regretfully. There was so much I wanted to know as I left the woodland and headed down the trail to the village.

4

Chapter 2

It was late afternoon when I had awakened. My sleep was peaceful unlike that which I had been experiencing. I laid in bed experiencing the brightness of the sun as it came through my window. The light threw off a sparkle as it penetrated the crystal hanging from the middle of the window curtain rod. The light was dispersed in various brilliant colors and shapes. The reflections bounced around on my blankets. I reached for them remembering the experiences of the night before. Tila. I was remembering the wonder of that beautiful fairy. I could picture her delicate structure and the opal essence of her wings. Her voice, the soft, strange sound that was also strong, bold and caring. Her eyes were green, like the moss near the waterfall. Maybe there was a touch of blue. They seemed large for her face. Her verbose manner sounded educated, she demonstrated a bit of mischief, yet spontaneous. I asked myself, was this real?" Perhaps it was a dream conjured up in the mind like a child longing for a friend. A fabrication, an illusion to overcome an emptiness from within. Maybe a desire to share what otherwise would go unheard. I will go to the forest again tonight. I push off the blankets attempting to start my day.

Deep in the woodland, Tila awakens. The sweet smell of honeysuckle fills the air as she breathes deep, yawning and stretching. She wipes the sleep from her eyes as she stands. The bees are busy collecting the sweet nectar from the honeysuckle flowers around her. They scatter as she makes her presence known to them. Tila, laid back down again, and snuggles herself back into the soft bed of flora and fauna. The bees returned to their task of collecting the nectar from the flowers. Tila is caught up in remembrance of the night and her encounter with the human. "Nicodemus." She says his name out loud. "Nicodemus" she repeats it again and again as if trying to decode how it sounds best. She says, "Nic, Nicky, Demus." Then, "Nicky, I shall call him Nicky." Then she says, loudly, "Hello! Nicky." Then a smile big enough to show the dimples on her cheeks flashed across her face. She flushed, stood up and greeted the bees and flew off to the pond to freshen up for the day. Washing her face, the questions begin to spin in her mind. She wondered what Nicky does in this place where he lives? What does he eat" Can he fly" Were his wings hidden in his coverings? She recalled that his eyes were blue. He was handsome, and he was very large. So many questions.

She began to get hungry so she flew off to find a fresh batch of berries and other fruit. She began to look forward to her adventures of the day. She also started to plan the time she would share with Nicky. She thought of his size and supposed if he couldn't fly, that could be a problem. It could slow the travel time down. These were things Tila would try to find answers to. Nicky made her feel good and a friend was something she too had longed for. She must go speak to Toiga, the eldest and wisest fairy. Tioga lives alone, beyond the waterfall in the cliff where the great bird nests. Guardian to the fairies. He knew Tila as he had spoken to her on occasion when he would come down from the cliffs to gather herbs and roots for his cures and special potions. Tioga was very old, all the fairies loved and revered him. He carried a cane made of vines twisted together with spun silk and it was adorned with many colorful stones and crystals. He always seemed to be mumbling or speaking to himself, which Tila found to be very funny. In fact that is what caught her attention when she first met him. She had giggled so loudly she gave her hiding place away and after a fashion they became friends. A smile touched her face as she recalled that moment long ago. Yes! That is what I must do" she said to herself, and off she went.

Evan the forest looked so much different. Today was the beginning of his weekend so he was not pressed for time, and thought he would relax some today. His mind kept wandering to last night's adventure and Tila, as he walked down the street he came across a store that was known for jewelry and small trinkets. Displayed in the window was a pendant that was decorated with opals and intricate engraving as he looked closer. The engraving was what looked to be a fairy but it was a butterfly amongst some flowers that appeared to be daisies. Going inside Nicodemus began to browse around. Noticing many different beautiful objects. Enclosed in a case lined with Black crushed velvet cloth, setting upon a pearl laced tray was a very tiny charm bracelet upon the bracelet was a wood carving shaped like a fairy and detailed with paint, it was very nice. Nicodemus stood suddenly startled, by the lady at the counter she asked from behind him if there was anything he needed help with, upon inquiring as to the cost Nick purchased it and left. Saying thank you and carefully placing the box with the bracelet in his pocket.

As he walked down the sidewalk he looked in the window of the card shop and noticed cards with fairies on them, how odd he thought I had never noticed such an abundance of fairytale and fairy items. Making his way to the park he sat upon the bench and dosed off contemplating the excitement that was building up in him and how he looked forward to seeing Tila tonight. As Tila reached the height to where Tioga lived she called out his name. There was no answer, she called and in a frumpy tone he replied "who is there". It is me Tioga, Tila I have come to speak with you. It must be important to you if you have come to my dwelling do come in, upon entering Tila was overwhelmed by the smell of herbs and spices which put an aura of calmness and reassurance to the place.

Surprisingly to her this was a tidy little place and most certainly dry and cozy when one needed such a place. Excuse the mess Tioga said I have been busy today drying and storing my herbs. What brings you up here my child? I have met someone Tila says with a hint of excitement in her voice! He said he was "human"! Quickly Tioga turns looking at Tila causing her to step back with some concern. I am sorry to startle you my child, it is just I have not heard that word in such a subtle manner before, and I am curious as to how you met him. You may sit down and explain to me if you like, as he sat Tila began to explain the event that took place the night of last, she also explained how she had watched him on his other ventures to the forest sitting and contemplating his life. How she had picked up on his feelings and his emptiness, and longing as Tioga sat there rubbing his jaw making sounds in reply to her conversation. She began to inquire about her concerns of travel and the size of this human that called himself man.

When she finished Tioga just sat there Tila became concerned then Tioga stood and walked to a shelf that was full of word boxes and began to thumb through them. Talking to himself saying, "interesting, huh, mmm" oh yes often what seemed like a long period of time he turned to Tila as he paced the floor he questioned Tila, do you wish to share these things of our world with him? Oh yes Tila replied. And do you feel that you can trust him with this world which has always been our own and not Just yours but the rest of our lives "I do" she replied. "Then" Tioga said, `` I would like for you to consider this from deep within your heart, and if you so choose to! Here is a vile which contains a potion that when applied will allow him to become the size we are and capable of flying, jumping up Tila grabbed Tioga tightly wrapping her arms around him and kissing him on the cheek "but" Tioga said, this will only last temporally at the first fading star of dawn the potion will wear off.

Thank you Tila joyfully said as she headed to the doorway! "Be careful," Tioga said, as a warning! Be sure you can trust him before you offer this opportunity to him. I promise Tila said as she flew off and away. Joyfully singing a song to herself while whistling the melody. Tioga listened as the sound faded away.

Chapter 3

Nicodemus awoke to the sounds of children scurrying through the park, upon realizing where he was he looked at the tower clock in the park, realizing it would not be long and he would be able to return to the forest. Getting up from the bench at which he sat, Nicodemus checked his pocket for the bracelet he had purchased earlier. It was still there, scurrying home Nicodemus figured he had time to clean up and prepare, for what he was not certain. What he was sure of was the feeling of joy that he had felt in the presents of Tila, and how he was at ease around her as well as the environment that was unfamiliar to him after he had eaten the berry. What if she was not real? What if she did not show up? It was something he did not even want to consider for that would be an empty feeling. He was sure in his mind that it was real and she would be there. Nicodemus began to think of questions he wanted to ask Tila. Mostly about her world and what adventures there were to experience and yet deep inside he knew he just wanted to share the company of someone to talk with, that made him feel less alone than he had in a long time, in a place that he had come to know as peaceful.

The light of the moon began to shadow the trail as Nicodemus started toward the edge of the forest, a trip he had made many times before, but never with the eagerness he felt now. It seems to escalate with every step. He noticed the only sound he was aware of was the beat of his heart, as his mind wrestled with the question of would she be there or not, as he reached the tree line he stopped to lean against a tree, catching his breath he stepped forward into the shadowed forest. The moon was rising quickly as he worked his way toward the area of the pond. He noticed that there was not one sound to be heard, was he in the right spot? It was as if all of the sudden he was lost but not Everything looked the same there before him was the rock he was sure he had sat on just the evening before.

Panic began to overwhelm him, with his eyes he searched frantically for something he would recognize anything that said this was the right spot. But nothing. Suddenly it was like his legs went weak and it became hard to focus. Sitting on the rock he laid his face in his hands sad not believing it was an illusion he was sure it was real. Maybe he was so excited he walked off the path he had taken last night "what should I do? " he asked himself. As he contemplated leaving the forest and starting over he began to hear a sound: it was the creatures of the night, it was the same lovely sound he recalled from the night of last.

A warm breeze caressed his hair, as he lifted his head from the palms of his hands. There it was next to him, the pond just as it was beautiful and sparkling the moon glowing brightly off the surface. As his eyes focused on the forest around him he heard Tilas voice, "hello Nicky". "You made it". He said with a doubtful assurance I am so glad to see you. As I am to see you said Tila but the pond this place was not here a few minutes ago. When I sat on this rock there was nothing but me, this rock and trees. I told you, Tila said this is a secret place for only the pure of heart and mind. Your belief brought it to life as well as you believing in me and what you saw last night. "I had some reservations," said Nicky! Yes, but you wanted it to be real with your heart and mind, now I know you are to be trusted. Replied Tila.

I am pleased that you trust me Tila. I would never mean to do you no harm. Good said Tila I have a question to ask you! What is it? How would you like to be my size and be able to fly the same as I do? It would only be temporary; the potion will only last until the fading of the first star at dawn! Then you would become as you are now! Will it be painful ask Nicodemus? I do not believe so replied

Tila but I really do not know. I have never seen it done before nor did Tioga tell me for I did not ask. Who is Tioga? He is a very wise and old fairy. Oh! Like a medicine man! What is a medicine man asked Tila. He is someone who heals the sick and can foresee the future. He too uses potions and herbs. Well kind of a guess said Tila but I am not sure about knowing the future. Will I be able to meet this Tioga? I think that might be possible. Tonight I would like to take you around my world and show you how I live. That sounds like a wonderful idea! When do we start, asked Nicodemus

Well anytime you are ready Nicky, Tila said by the way may I call you Nicky? You may! Said Nicodemus that is what my mother calls me! Is that bad? asked Tila, no! Said Nicky we are very close and that is good. I am pleased said Tila you will have to tell me about your mother sometime, yes I will said Nicky. Okay are you ready? Yes! Tila pulled the vile from the pouch at her hip pulling the moss plug off the top. She told Nicky to stay very still. Neither one being aware of what might accrue. They being overly careful but content at the task at hand as Tila pulled the top off the vial a crystal pearl mist began to rise. It looked like glitter, the color of the rainbow began to make its way downward. Tila began to fly around Nicodemus head as she flew she spoke out the magical words. Oh mystical mist with sparkling rain, give unto Nicky fairy essence to gain, give him Wing Sturdy and Strong, and unto him a heart that belongs. As he gained his sight threw the berry, allowing him the body in this world like a fairy. By this time Nicky had closed his eyes feeling dizzy from watching Tila go around his head over and over, faster and faster, till she was a sparkling blur.

He listened as she spoke, waiting for something to happen but he felt nothing, was it going to work he was not sure but he hoped it would. Deep in his heart there was no doubt, saying to himself I want to change, I want to change, exhausted Tila stopped circling Nicky and she landed on the rock somewhat off balance. Taking a deep breath she looked into the mist that was setting around where Nicky was, she could not see him. Looking down there on the side of the rock was Nicky. She jumped down and called his name! Nicky

Nicky open your eyes. Feeling somewhat disappointed for he had not felt a change to lift his head from his hands. There before him was the most beautiful pair of green eyes he had ever seen, and hair the color of gold like he had never believed possible. She was as large as he was, her skin was smooth as silk and her lips and cheeks were rosy red. She was dressed with rose petals and smelled of honeysuckles. It worked Tila said with enthusiasm that made Nicky take a step back.

What he said! "It worked," she again replied. Nicky began to look around and everything was very large. How could it be he had not felt anything yet as he surveyed his surroundings there was a definite change. He rubbed his hands over his forehead and they stopped just past the hair line. What? He said, startled! As he realized he had something protruding from his head and noticed that they were very sensitive to the touch. What are they? He asked excitedly, he said, they are antennas, Tila said. I did change! Do I have wings, can I fly, what do I do? How do I make my wings work? He began spinning around and around trying to see his wings but without success. He fell to the ground as he made himself dizzy. Tila began to laugh hysterically rolling on the ground kicking her feet. As her laughter calmed to a giggle they both stood. Trying to compose himself what is so funny Nicky asked somewhat embarrassed, you looked like a squirrel chasing his tail, they both began to laugh!

Taking Nicky's hand Tila said follow me! Her touch was like silk just as he had thought and she led him a few feet away to the edge of the pond. Look into the pond and you will be able to see your reflection. As Nicky looked into the water he could see the antennas reaching from his head. Leaning forward he saw them, there on his back were wings just like those that were on Tilas back, beautiful and radiant. Large in size as it seemed as if they glittered with a life of their own. Speechless at what he saw he stepped back looking at Tila trying to speak but the words would not come out. You make a very beautiful fairy said Tila, impressed and somewhat shy. She began to see him a little differently now that he was not so big. His frame was built well, his eyes were light blue with curly brown hair. Yes he certainly looked different standing there with a leaf shaped like a pair of shorts. Wow! It seemed like the easiest thing for Nicky to say. What do you want to do? asked Tila. How do I fly? Said Nicky. Concentrate on your wings and make them go back and forth.

Nicky closed his eyes and put all his thoughts into his wings. Squeezing his hand in a ball he tried but nothing. Relax Tila said think about your shoulders and think about the motions the wings make, as Tila moved her wings to show him. Again he thought of his wins and flying. There they moved as he thought of what they were doing his wings opened up then closed keeping his mind on his wings. They began to move with more frequency back and forth. Soon he could feel a slight breeze as the wings seemed to work on their own, at least with less concentration. Soon he felt light on his feet and noticed his body had risen some but he couldn't quite get off the ground. Maybe if he jumped up a little, but that did not seem to work either. He turned to the rock and began to climb. "What are you doing"! Asked Tila. Maybe if I get some height and jump I will fly. Be careful Tila said. I will Nicky said as he reached the top of the rock as he walked to the edge of the rock he began to move his wing back and forth faster and faster. Soon he could feel himself light footed and lifting slightly off the ground to his surprise he began to lift. Tila hollered up your doing it your doing it!! Now lean forward. As Nicky leaned forward he began to move off the rock forward towards the pond. Excitedly he turned to Tila, look I'm doing it! and as he lost his concentration and fell into the pond, causing water to splash onto the shore and Tila who was respectfully holding back her laughter and at the same time concerned if Nicky was alright. As he rose from the water he was ecstatic. I did it! I did it! With a big smile. Tila could not hold it back no longer and knowing he was alright she began to laugh out loud saying yes you did. as he crawled to the bank with water dripping from his soaked self they sat down next to each other and laughed long and hard. I can do it! Nicky said "yes you can reply Tila.

Chapter 4

As the two of them sat there sharing the events of Nicky's comical first flying experience all became dark as the moon seemed to disappear. Nicodemus became frightened he did not know what was going on. As Tila looked up she told Nicky. "Do not be afraid" it is only Brier. Brier, who is Brier? Asked Nicky he is the wisest creature of the forest at night and he sees all that goes on. Looking up all he saw was wings as the wind blew hard as Brier landed on the rock where the two sat. He will not harm us asked Nicky, being somewhat frightened and vulnerable Not being used to the change that had transpired or being so small next to something he had always been larger than even as a child. That would certainly take some getting used to. No he will not hurt us replied Tila as Brier landed he said Hoo! Hoo! Tila introduced Nicky to Brier explaining all that had happened when she was done. Brier looked at Nicky and spoke. I am aware of what you are, and if Tila believes you are worthy of such a chance then I trust her judgment and I am pleased to meet you.

I heard all the commotion and came to investigate when I saw it was you Tila and someone I was unfamiliar with I thought I would come to introduce myself. Sorry if I startled you Nicky! This must be very different for you, yes very much so said Nicodemus. Tila explained how she was helping Nicky use his wings to fly and how he had fallen into the pond. This brought a chuckle from Brier. Who then suggested a trial flight in the middle of his back for he had to make his evening rounds. Appreciatively they both agreed without hesitation. As Brier jumped to the ground he said climb on. It was clear Tila had done this before she had flown upon Brier back and helped Nicky up by sitting him behind her she showed him how to hold on. Turning she then told Brier they were ready. With a hop they were off and flying! Not exactly what they had in mind, but they were flying. Brier flight was silent as they quickly covered ground things began to look smaller as they flew higher. Never had Nicky imagined such a view; they were high above the trees now and Nicky pointed out the glowing lights of the village a short distance from the forest.

How beautiful even Tila never flew this high very often. Tila pointed out various areas, such as the waterfall where Tioga lived and the great bird which Nicky explained was an eagle. The flower fields, and crystal river that actually sparkled like a trail of diamonds. Looking up at the stars it was as if you could reach up and pocket one. Well if one had pockets, thought Nicky. The air was so clean and fresh yet cooler than on the forest floor. All of the sudden Brier began to dive downward making side circling turns The tree tops keep coming closer and closer. Brier turns to ask Tila where she would like to be let off. She began to speak but looking up all she could get out of her mouth was watch out for the tree! Doing the only thing he could, Brier turned sharply and down. As he did so, Nicky lost his grip and began falling downward. Tila gasped as she heard Nicky scream something aloud but turning she saw he was gone. Pulling at Brier he turned as they did; they both saw Nicky turning as he continued to plummet to the forest below.

Brier flapped his wings twice, gaining speed directly for Nicky, encouraged desperately by Tila. As Nicky fell he was noticing the speed to which he was headed to the ground below. What could he do! As Tila came closer Nicky could hear both her and Brier flap your wings!! Flap your wings!!! My wings! oh yes my wings. Nicky was so afraid he had forgotten all about the wings he now had. He began concentrating as he could feel the movement in his back. The wings began to expand and contract, over and over he began flapping them back and forth his momentum downward began to slow. Nicky opened his wings and began to glide. Soon he was awkwardly swaying from side to side but gliding non the less he was flying! Tila said thank you and good-by as she left Briers back. Brier said good luck as he flew off among the treetops by the time Tila caught up with Nicky he was smiling from ear to ear. Look Tila he said I'm flying! Yes you are but be careful. As he began to move parts of his body he noticed he could change directions right or left up or down. Before too long he was doing half circles and Banking from side to side.

He would never guess this could be so much work. Then it dawned on him how he was going to land, that is something else he had never done before! Tila encouraged him every step of the way, being careful not to Entangle each other. Nicky asked Tila how he was supposed to land. Starting to giggle she caught herself and explained that as you get closer to the ground you point your feet down and move your wings faster to cause an air cushion then the next thing you know you've landed! It sounds easy enough though Nicky But then again that's what he thought when it came to the idea of flying and look how that went yet here he was flying! That was great for now!

As Tila coached Nicky in the technique of flight they had covered a great deal of ground. Seeing the pond up ahead, Nicky was ready to take a rest; he was very tired from his endeavors. As they got closer to the pond they headed straight for the shore. With a tilt of his wings he slowed to a hover and gently touched the earth. With Tila landing next to him he turned wrapping his arms around her neck and said thank you. That was so very wonderful. In fact that was the most exciting thing I have ever done!

Tila caught off guard smiled and told Nicky how proud she was of him. Together they sat near the pond glad to be safe and very happy that Nicky had flown. Nicky was soon eager to try flying again. While walking around he would practice moving his wings. Soon he was making short flights around the pond, Tila began to follow him giving pointers here and there to enhance his ability, before he knew it Nicky was leading Tila deeper into the forest as he flew he noticed a sensation of awareness he was not familiar with almost like a pain in his head. Blam!! He had stopped mid-flight struck he could not move as Tila hovered near him. She told him not to struggle, it would only bring big trouble, what kind of trouble? Nicky asked! As he began to feel afraid then she saw it big black and hungry looking. As Nicky looked he saw the biggest spider he had ever seen and in such detail. He tried to pull his arms or legs free but it was no use. As the spider crawled closer to Nicky Tila screamed so loud that it hurt Nicky's ears, and also made the spider stop. Tila tried to help Nicky get free but it only tangled him more to the webbing, made for such a purpose. Nicky knew how they wrapped t heir catch to eat. No he was definitely afraid. As was Tila, what could she do? She turned and started heading back the way they had come. Where are you going? Cried out Nicky!

Please don't leave me here! I will help you, replied Tila as she turned flying as fast as she could headed straight for Nicky Bam! She slams head into Nicky's chest and the spider leaps forward the web breaks causing them both to lay upside down against the web stuck! As the spider came closer they felt it was over. Scream! Yelled Nicky screamed loud! Maybe we can scare him. But it only seemed to entice the spider more, one more step and it was over. With a hard crash and a gust of wind Nicky and Tila found themselves rolling on the ground. Coming to a stop and sitting up, they began to check themselves than each other. They were all there. What happened! One minute they were food and the next here they sat soon it became very apparent what happened! Are you all right" they both looked startled there high on the branch of a tree was Brier, I heard you screaming and it seemed as if I showed up just in time.

Yes you did said Tila thank you was all Nicky could manage your are welcome my friends be more careful call if you need help and off Brier flew leaving them both sitting there thankful to be alive. As they headed to the pond Nicky began to feel funny noticing Tila looked up, the stars were fading as they reached the pond Nicky changed back to a man. What a night Tila said as she flew up to Nicky. Yes it was I am sorry it came to an end it is not over just temporarily delayed yes delayed Nicky said as they sat on the rock to say goodbye!

Chapter 5

Morning came early for Nicodemus although it was no surprise that he could not sleep with all that had happened throughout the night it was really a wonder he even tried. What a feeling being so small and flying how could one even begin to explain how that felt. The sights such freedom sure he was not the best but what an experience and flying on an owl" I mean really! Nicodemus said out loud. As he moved his pants from the bed he remembered the bracelet he had purchased yesterday. He had forgotten all about it; there was just too much going on. I will give it to her tonight, he thought!. Just the thought brought a rejuvenating energy to him, Nicodemus began tidying up his house for the third time since he had been home. Meanwhile in the forest Tila layed restless in a bed of cat paw flowers, their softness matched only by the cotton from the cotton trees.

Hidden from the creatures of the day she caught glimpses of bird overhead darting swiftly and accurately through the trees. She recalled Nicky darting back and forth as he began to gain some control over his wings. That enlarged the smile that seemed to be even present since they had parted for the day. She recalled how fortunate they had been that Brier had heard their calls and rescued them from the spider's web, and how afraid she became when Nicky had fallen from Brier's back.

But most of all she would never forget his first flight right into the pond, that still made her want to laugh out loud. And how handsome he was as a fairy or was it because he was her size his features seem to be more attractive. Although he had been all along. There was no doubt she couldn't wait to see him again. What adventures would that hold? She would have to go see Tioga again but that would be later as she thought about Nicky. Tila held a smile as she fell fast asleep.

Returning from town Nicky walked from the front door to the kitchen table where he began going through the sacks of merchandise he had purchased.

Among this stuff was necessities for the household. Food and among the small bags that sat there were a couple of pictures he would hang upon the wall. One of which was a forest scene with mushrooms, flowers, a waterfall and little fairies, not like he knew of but it was lovely. There were a couple of postcards, one which he would send to his sister, the other would go to his mother, and last but not least. A small delicate silver music box. That played the tune of Twinkle, twinkle, little star and was adorned with a half moon and stars a few of them were as if shooting across the sky. This he picked up at a craft store and was made to go into a doll house as a hope chest. I hope you will like this also Tila, you will be able to put your bracelet in it.

Nicodemus said out loud to himself, after putting things away Nicodemus walked to the window staring out to the forest. Growing late in the afternoon Tila was awakened by the sound of a woodpecker working frantically to retrieve insects and bugs from within the tree's bark. Rolling off of the catspaw she stood yawning, and stretching well wiping the sleep from her eyes, lazily she wondered to the collective of early morning dew still captive at the base of a wildflower, splashing her face, she ran her fingers through her hair. Pulling apart the matted curls from laying to one side as she slept. I must first find Tioga, she thought to herself and off she flew being careful to not be seen by the creatures of the day that might mistake her for food.

Reaching the entrance way to Tiogas dwelling she called out no answer. She called out again with still no answer now where he could be" she wondered if she would check the usual spots and see if she could locate him. There was one place left! And off to the wild berry patch she headed. Tila heard Tioga well before she saw him, with a half chuckle she called out to Tioga where are you? As she listened she no longer heard Tioga talking to himself. She called out again, then he answered over here, as she found her way to him Tioga was complaining about the plumpness of the berries and how he wished there had been more rain for this time of season. It looks as though you have been busy Tioga! By the look of the extra pack you carry you have been well successful. "Oh yes" "very much so" was his reply. But it tends to get tiresome on the weak old bones. You are not old! replied Tila, being respectful and polite. Why thank you he said, then asked how are you today Tila? And how is your new found friend, he asked while sitting on a nearby mushroom. Tila joined him and began telling of yesterday's adventures, Tioga had fallen off his mushroom when he heard the one about falling into the pond. I wish I would have been there he said as he repositioned himself back on the mushroom I am sensing you would like to spend more time with this Nicky! Correct "yes" Tila said, in fact I was going to ask if I may have some more potion. And if possible to see if Nicky could come and say hello to you he had asked last night.

And I told him I would find out, well commented Tioga it sounds to me as if you two are getting along very well. And I suspect if Nicky is going to be around, and part of our world on occasion I should meet with him. When do you plan on seeing him again? Tonight Tila said with a smile, well now! Tioga replied with a slight sarcastic smile. Tila was kind of blushed but held it back hoping he hadn't noticed. I am glad to hear you say that! When can we come by asked Tila well how about this evening about suppertime. That would be very nice, thank you, Tila said. And the potion! Well that is simple Tioga said all you have to do is repeat the magical words and he will change as he had done before. Oh thank you! Thank you very much. Now I must get going, said Tioga. I must get home and tidy up and prepare supper. Could I get you to help me with one of my bags? It will save me a trip, why yes it would be a pleasure they both grabbed a bag and off they went.

Chapter 6

Nicky took his last few steps before entering the forest, to control his excitement and to make sure he had not forgotten the bracelet and music box that was a present for Tila. He was hoping she would enjoy them and not find them too material. He had never bought anything for a fairy before. He thought with a smile, as he walked to their meeting spot Nicky began to recall all he could about flying! He too could not help but to laugh some as he clearly recalled flying off the rock into the pond.

He also recalled how sweet Tila laughter sounded and how pleasant it was to see her rolling on the ground hysterically. Also the sincerity of her concern both when he had fallen and when she tried to help him at the spider web. How his heart melted when he thought of the tragedy of being eaten by that same spider and the helplessness. He would try to be more careful this time for Tilas sake! Tila watched as Nicky approached, she was pleased to see him and thought of how different he looked in his natural form. And largely she had thought of what it would be like to be human. Yet she had no idea what his world was about; she had only seen it from afar when she would ride on Brier's back, and that was mostly lights and a time or two when she would see rolling carts. She would ask Nicky about his world. Hello Tila Nicky said as he approached the rock he had come to know as their spot. As he sat next to where Tila was he asked her how she was. She said "I am fine Nicky, it is good to see you. I was just wondering what it was like to be human and be a part of your world, would you tell me about the females of your world. Well as Nicky did not know where to start, he said "the females of my world are not much different than you. They come in all shapes and sizes depending on nationality, different colored eyes and hair. Of course they don't have wings or antennas and they are not as small as you but there is a surprising similarity in both human and fairys

Do men take females as their mates or companions? We do not take them per say but when a man and woman have common interest and enjoy each other's company they spend a good deal of time together sometimes they marry. Marry? Asked Tila "Yes, marry the joint for life. I understand fairies join when they feel compatible with one another. Are the women pretty? asked Tila, yes some wear makeup. Stuff that colors their face and does things to their hair to change its appearance. Do you have a mate? Tila asked not sure all of the sudden if she wanted to know the answer. "No," he said. The answer came so quick he startled himself. Eagerly Tila changed the subject and with some sarcasm and a smile asked Nicky if he was ready to fly again? He began to say yes when he remembered the music box and bracelet. First he said I have something I bought for you with surprise Tila said you have something for me?

Yes as he set the music box and the bracelet on the rock Tila's eyes showed the grateful surprise that she felt. As she lifted the bracelet it was apparent it would not fit on her wrist but she put it over her head and it made a perfect necklace. It is beautiful she said with a crackle in her voice she began to walk around the shiny box commenting excitedly about the moon and stars and how it sparkled in the moonlight it is also very beautiful, what is it she asked. Nicky told her to open it. As she stood next to the box it came about halfway to her knees. When she lifted the lid she stumbled back off the rock as the sound came from the box. She flew back up to it and noticed the inside was a bright red and very soft. It is a music box Nicky said the music is from a song called Twinkle twinkle little star. Tila asked what the words were to the music. Nicky began to sing it as best he could. "Twinkle Twinkle Little Star, how I wonder where you are! up above the sky so dark, like a candle in the sky. I hope to see you with my eyes. He was sure it was not right but it was as close as he could remember.

"That is wonderful," Tila said. As she closed the lid the music stopped. Nicky said I am "ready". Tila turned, forgetting about the change from human to fairy till she noticed she had to look up to see him. Oh!! Yes she said well sit right here and close your eyes. As Nicky closed his eyes Tila began circling him reciting the magic words. Oh mystical mist with sparking rain, give unto Nicky fairy essence to gain, give him wings sturdy and strong and unto him a heart that belongs. As he gained his sight threw the berry, allowing him to body in this world like a fairy. When Tila stopped just like before as the mist cleared he was not as large as he had once been.

It worked again! Nicky was small and he had wings. "Well" Nicky said, obviously more content with the change this time as opposed to last. What do you want to do tonight? Nicky asked as he made his wings move back and forth. Lifting himself off the ground flying upon the rock he tried to look as if he did it all along, a little surprised that he seemed to be picking it up so well. Tila said follow me as she flew out over the pond, as she did she called back to Nicky. "Don't fall in" and began to giggle. Nicky was impressed at the ease and comfort at which flying seemed to be this time he passed Tila saying catch me if you can. They darted in and out of trees, hollow fallen logs, bushes and up and down cliff faces. As they come to the waterfall Tila said Nicky follow me and will go see Tioga is it alright asked Nicky. Yes I spoke with him today and he invited us to come by for super.

I am feeling a little hungry now that you mention it. As they flew up the face of the cliff Nicky could feel the mist off the waterfall, the sound ot made was like a train approaching from the distants a low rumbling roar. Everything he had seen was so beautiful, untampered, natural and undisturbed! Man had a way of destroying most everything around him, and usually replacing it with something unnatural or fabricated, to look around him he could only sigh to himself. As they reached the ledge high on the cliff Tila called out to Tioga, come on in i have been waiting for you, super is on the table said Tioga. As they entered Nicky was introduced to Tioga who politely took his hand and welcomed him to his home. Thank you for inviting me to your home and your table said Nicky as he relaxed some.

The smell was also soothing; it reminded him of the shop in the village where they sold incense, candles, potpourri and herbal medicines. Please have a seat and make yourself comfortable. I will get us some tea. Why thank you Tila and Nicky replied as they took a seat at the table. Tioga said it is a pleasure to finally meet you Nicky I have heard so much about you from Tila. I feel as though I have known you for as long as she has. Thank you said Nicky I would also like to thank you for the opportunity to be a part of your world in a manner befitting. How is your flying going? I understand you made quite the splash as your first time out, they all chuckled as Nicky said he felt more at ease and in control. Yes he is doing much much better, replied Tila almost feeling somewhat left out of the conversation. She then asked if there was anything she could do to help as Tioga brought the tea. It is honey tea with a touch of peppermint. I hope you like it.

Nicky noticed the cups were made of what look to be tulips with a leaf base and small branch for a handle. On the table was honey and an assortment of berries, fruits, nuts and seeds. Please help yourself, Tioga said, taking a seat across the table. As they ate Tioga said there are many things I would like to speak with you about Nicky, but I believe you and Tila have plenty of things to do and when that is so. Time just does not stand still, so you both have fun and we'll talk another time. The conversation was more about the weather and the gathering of berries and fruit and of course the lack of rain. After relaxing from the meal everyone feeling quite satisfied, Tila suggested that they be going, as they prepared to leave they all said their goodbyes and made arrangements to visit again going out the door Nicky and Tila waved goodbye and flew down toward the forest floor. Flying through the mist of the waterfall Tila asked Nicky what he would like to do. I would like to go to the river we flew over the other night when we were on Brier's back, it looked as if it were like a river of stars.

Throwing brilliant sparkles of light everywhere. Okay Tila said follow me off they went. Nicky was enjoying the sights that passed below him as he flew. They soon reached the river, and as the view from above it sparkled and put out a radiant glow the water seemed calm enough and so clear you could see the bottom clearly the moonlight seemed to bounce off the rocks below. It was as if someone had polished all of the contents within, Nicky asked Tila if she had ever floated down it before. What on the water she said did not quit getting his meaning. I mean like on a log or raft "no" I can't say I have she replied. Nicky began looking then he had an idea there on the river he saw a leaf fall and began to float down the slow moving current. Then it dawned on him! "A big leaf"! "what ", Tila said. A big leaf, if we get a big enough leaf we can float down the river. That sounds like a wonderful idea Tila said, she mostly flies everywhere, so a new way of travel would be fun to try, as Nicky looked around that was it.! Just on the other side of the river is a plant that has leaves like a banana tree that was just what he was looking for, very large, solid wide and shaped just right. Follow me Tila I will need your help. They flew right to the plant landing next to it he said to Tila this is just what we need now if it floats off well go! They both got on one side of the leaf and began to pull the harder they pulled the further the leaf bent toward them. Soon it was a struggle just a little more Nicky said. SNAP! With a loud cracking sound the leaf broke free causing Nicky and Tila to tumble backwards rolling over and landing next to each other on their rear ends oops! Said Nicky asking Tila if she was alright? With a quizzical smile on his face "yes I am" she replied.

Now all we got to do is pull it toward the river which was only a few feet away grabbing it by the stem. They pulled it toward the edge of the river, turning it over and over and pushing it easily into the water. As it hits the water it begins to turn with the slow moving current. Hop on Nicky says as he reaches for Tilas hand. She grabs his hand and leaps on the leaf. The leaf rocks a little but stays afloat and holds both their weight. They are off, wow! Tila says as she settles on the leaf I have never done this before it is a lot different than flying or riding on Jazmin or Brier. Who is Jazmin? Jazmin is the guardian of the forest floor, she is a puma she told me. A puma! Nicky said, shocked. Why do you look shocked? Tila asked, because a puma is a big cat and a cougar they are feared even by humans. Oh there is nothing to fear, she is the most friendly. Sometimes I ride on her back as she wanders the forest and we talk. Oh, said Nicky I would like to meet her someday. I hope you will reply to Tila. As they floated down the river they saw many different creatures coming to the water's edge to drink. TIla would wave to some of them and they would wave back.

Then there on the bank Nicky saw a raccoon look he said pointing to the shore, oh yes Tila said hello Justin! As he looked up he replied hello! Tila what are you doing on the leaf" this is my friend Nicky and we are afloat down river! How's the fishing Tila asked? I have finished my meal Tila. I was just washing up! You'll have to come by and see my latest gathering. Tila replied. Well see you later! Okey said Justin as he returned to washing himself. Nicky could hear it before he saw it. What is that said Tila Nicky had noticed that the water had taken on a new flow? It was beginning to ripple then they saw it. Can you swim? He asked Tila yes I can but we can fly away! Oh no! said Nicky that is part of the fun it is called riding the rapids. The water was much faster with 2-3 foot waves. HOLD ON NICKY SAID.

Chapter 7

Soon they began to travel at greater speed and the leaf started rocking up and down side to side. Tila asked shall we leave now!? Sensing some fear from Tila Nicky said it will be alright I can swim like a fish. I will not let anything happen to you! It is meant to be exciting and thrilling. Okay said Tila! Just scoot behind and hold on just like we are on Briers back. Eagerly she put her arms around his waist and held on. Just in time as the leaf shot upward the water had disappeared Tila squeezed tight, as she gasped out loud wow! Nicky hallowed out as they shut down again this time Tila screamed "oh no"!!! All she could see was water rushing and spinning. The motion began to lift her stomach. As they began to go sideways and up water splashed all over them they were soaked. As fast as it started it began to slow and the water smoother Tila was still squeezing hard around Nicky's waist with her eyes closed. Nicky noticed and smiled, as he said out loud "that was great". Tila opened her eyes and asked if they were okay, yes he said as he paddled to the shore line and getting off he helped Tila to shore. Were she sat glad to be off the water, are you okay? Nicky asked, yes I am!. Just not quite sure what to think of it. Nicky laid back letting Tila take a break before he began to ponder any further adventures.

Kicking back they looked up at the stars. Tila began thinking about the bracelet as she reached for her neck, feeling it hanging near her bosom, and the musical box that Nicky had brought her. It made such a beautiful sound, she had never had anything so special. And the sound like she had never heard the likes of.

Some of the words came to mind as she looked into the sky. "Twinkle Twinkle Little Star" the rest of the words she could not recall but tried to hum the melody to herself. What would I like to do next? asked Nicky turning towards Tila. they heard the panic crys. Help me! Help me! As they turned to face the coming sound they saw a field mouse being chased by a kit fox. Help me! Help me Tila! The cry a panic, Some 50 yards off slam the fox jumped on the mouse pinning him to the ground with a force that was obviously painful. Get off me you brat! The mouse said to the fox. As Nicky watched it, he was horrified that the fox was going to eat that poor helpless mouse. You stop it right now Nicky hollered with authority. Forgetting his size. Do not harm that mouse, as he finished Tila turned to Nicky its alright that is cheal and Huey they will not harm each other. They alway fight, Tila had turned to the two and headed toward them, they had stopped startled by the command of the strange and unknown voice. Cheal was still on Huey get off me you big brat! Get off me I can't breath, gasping for air Heuy continued to struggle. What's going on here Tila asked Cheal begin to explain his side of the story as he stepped off Huey trying to put on a totally innocent look. I was minding my own business listening to the sound of a frog Hopping around the river I was going to catch him and Huey kept. Being noisy, I asked him to quit. That's not true Huey said butting in I wasn't doing nothing wrong yes you were said Cheal. We were walking through the forest and Cheal kept stepping on my tail so I turned around and kicked his foot because he was laughing at me. And he said he was going to eat me so I hit him again and ran away. So he started it, Huey said. That's not true. I wasn't doing anything he started by calling me names like fatso, stupid even when I was chasing him then he saw you Tila and acted like I was going to kill him. He is so phony. No I am not Huey said in his defense, now you both stop Tila said your both say your sorry. Hanging their heads they both apologized to one another. Tila had been through this a hundred times with these two; it was always theatrical and always explained with 2 or 3 different stories. Walking up to Tila Nicky asked "is everything alright"?

Yes it she replied Tila this is Cheal and Huey looking up they both said hello obviously feeling scolded. This is Nicky. He is a friend of mine. He thought you were trying to really harm each other. Oh no, said Huey. We argue all the time but we are like brothers. We are both single offspring and we have grown up together. Yea! Said Cheal I would never hurt Huey too bad. Even when he makes me very upset. We love each other. Cheal laid his head down and Huey climbed up. And off they went. Wow, Nicky said that was scary for a minute. I really thought that the fox was going to eat the mouse. No Tila said they always scramble. It's just sorta natural for them. They practically raised each other. Well what would you like to do now Tila asked if it is getting late we should go back to the pond, and put my music box up before Purdy finds it, who is Purdy Nicky asked. Purdy is a weasel who takes anything shiny that sparkles to where he takes it. I do not know but he does take it and the word he uses the most is Purdy. Purdy this, Purdy that, he is nice he just can't help himself from taking things

He is always taking from the crows who also love pretty stuff. Okay we better go then and off they went. Reaching the rock where they meet. They were pleased to see the music box still there., shining in the moonlight. It is so beautiful, Tila said. I will put it in a safe place if you will help me carry it to my secret cave. A secret cave Nicky said yes it is behind the waterfall Tioga showed it to me in case I ever needed a place to stay. I would be glad to help you, Nicky said. Well grab a handle and will go grabbing a handle they flew off toward the waterfall. It was a little awkward going but it was not all that heavy. Soon they reached the falls and about half way up they flew behind the water. And then some five feet wide was on opening! Going inside it was like a corridor some twenty feet long and there it opened up to a very large room.

Bigger than Nicky's house with no walls, here and there were layers of rock that looked like shelves and rock beds in one corner of the room was a beacon of light that shone from the ceiling. The waterfall was only about 50 feet tall. It was as if some humans lived here a long time ago. There were paintings on the wall and a hole where there were pieces of broken pottery and some that were not. Going to a remote corner of the cave was an area that Tila had adopted as her own little space. There were flowers and verbs she had gotten from Tioga. Food and a holding tank made of rock for water. Her bed was cotton from the cotton tree and odds and ends gathered for places to sit, often placing the music box in the selected spot they sat and began to talk about the day's adventures. As the talk Tila fell asleep and Nicky sat there admiring her beauty and being thankful to have a friend as her. The hour was late and he quietly left the cave and sat at the pond till he was able to go home.

Chapter 8

Tila woke sometime mid- morning. Looking around she called to Nicky but no answer. She then noticed the sun coming through the hole in the cave. She walked to the music box opening the lid and she began to dance around the room. Tending to the morning chores she began making up words to the melody. "Nicky, Nicky, where are you? I'm glad we met, how about you? I enjoy when we're together, I hope that you enjoy it too! The melody rang as it echoed through the cave. When she came to where Nicky was last at, she saw the flower he had placed where he was sitting down in the dirt was a smiling face. She reached up and held onto the necklace she wore, closing her eyes. She continued wistfully prancing from place to place hell! She heard! Hello, it's me Tioga. Do come in, she called out. Please "do come in" she closed the lid to the music box. Tioga came in saying good morning child! You seem to be in good spirits this day.

I take it all went well last night "oh yes" "very" said Tila we went floating down the river on a leaf! "On a leaf you say" yes we went down the rapids ``, Nicky called them, I was afraid and had my eyes closed but Nicky was excited. I wouldn't mind trying it again when she finished. I thought I heard some music as I came to the entrance, Replied Tioga. Oh yes! Come see! It is a music box and isn't it beautiful! Very much so said Tioga, how do you play it? I do not play it, it plays itself. She explained all you have to do is open the lid. Opening it as she said so, it began where it had left off. How nice it sounds Tioga said as he asked to sit and listen. Please do Tila said I'm sorry for my lack of manners. It's all right he said as he sat Tila rocked back and forth to the music and noticed Tioga did the same. After a few minutes the music came to a stop.

Tila looked shocked she did not expect it to stop like that. Tioga said, I have never heard such a thing from a box before. "Oh no"! Tila said, ``What is wrong asked Tioga. I don't know why it stopped, she answered. I hope it did not break! May I look closer asked Tioga of course you may she said as she walked to the box with him. Tioga began to inspect the box carefully; he noticed how intricate the detail was and how shiny! He could see himself as clear as looking into water. He moved one of the handles and it was solid to the box. As he walked to the other side. He tried the second handle but this time he was able to turn it as he did, it started to make music. But as he let go it stopped! Reaching over and turning the handle the other way it clicked the further he turned it the more it clicked. AS he let it go it played only for a moment though He reached over and turned it till it would turn no longer and it began to play. Oh thank you Tioga, Tila said relieved and with a sigh and a smile. I enjoy listening to it said Tioga. Anyway he said I came by to tell you I enjoyed his company and you are welcome to bring him anytime. Maybe we can pick some berries and herbs together one day. Yes, that would be a great idea. Just let me know when I have things to do so I'll be on my way. Have a nice day Tioga said "you to she replied and thank you for fixing my music box. Tila walked over and sat next to the box as it played on.

Nicky was sound asleep dreaming of flying when he heard the pounding on the door! Just a minute Nicky said and he looked around startled to gain his bearings and open his eyes a little: he pulled the covers and made his way to the door as again the loud pounding began! What is so urgent Nicky said as he opened the door. It was an inpatient boy standing there with a piece of paper in his hand. Telegram sir it seems to be urgent thank you young man! Taking the paper he began to read while shutting the door. URGENT-STOP MOTHER VERY ILL-Stop-REQUEST YOU PRESENT-STOP

A.S.A.P-STOP. Dr Polly stop. Oh Goodness! Nicky began to panic as he scurried through the house going many different directions and not really accomplishing a thing. Clothes, suitcase, secure house, money, wallet, all this was going through his head as he washed his face still trying to open his eyes. Clothes I must get dressed Nicky said as he began pulling on his pants, Darn! He said as he realized the zipper was in the back.

Turning his pants around he sat on the bed pulling his socks on and shoes he pulled the first shirts he grabbed on and put a couple more on the bed. Then some socks, pants, hygiene items, and grabbed his wallet keys and change off the dresser. Reaching up in the closet he grabbed his change jar for just such an emergency pulling the sash he put the jar back, locked the windows and started out the door as remembered his suitcase, retrieving it he stood by the door took one more look around. Shut the door and rush to the train station, may I have a ticket for the first train east. It will heave in ten minutes, he paid for his ticket and went to the gate marked (east bound) handed the conductor his ticket and got on board. He quickly stowed his suitcase in the seat next to him and tried to talk the train in motion. Come on he said over and over soon it jerked forward pulling the cars tight and began rolling down the track. He began thinking as to his mother's well being What could have happened? Is it so bad she might not make it and what of her craft shop? Will he have to stay to keep the business going? And his stuff that was left behind. LEFT BEHIND! Tila! OH NO! He said out loud causing everyone to turn to look at him.

There was no way of letting her know what was going on, he was so panicked it did not even cross his mind. He had to get to his mother tho. There was no choice what he was going to do? As the train rolled down the tracks Tila began preparing to meet with Nicky she would suggest going to the never ending salt lake. Where they could watch the big fish jump and play in the sand she would show him the pools of water that held the stars. And the retracting flowers that grow under water. And fish that look like porcupines and the water that reaches out trying to pull itself inland. Tila flies out of the cave and heads toward the pond. The night is cloudy and there is moisture in the air. Tila is aware that a storm is approaching and to a fairy that is a dangerous thing. The wind is impossible to fly in and the raindrops are big enough to harm something as small as a fairy. She will wait till Nicky shows up and suggest maybe just stay in the cave and talk.

They can go to the endless lake another time when it is nicer weather. The moon is beginning to set midway in the sky and Nicky has not shown. Tila began to wonder if everything is alright Nicky has always shown a little early. Could he be mad at her for falling asleep, No! Or he certainly would not have left the flowers, she knew there was no disagreement as it grew later she began to feel funny in her stomach something was not quite right she felt empty and alone. What could it be? The first drop of rain hit near Tila and the wind began to blow, as the moon was overcast by dark clouds. Tila knew she could not stay and wait as the weather was getting worse. She took one more look in the direction that Nicky came, nothing! she flew off to her cave, by the time she reached the entrance it was raining hard and the wind was bending the tops of the trees. Entering her home Tila shook off the chill and dried herself off. She was feeling very confused. And it seems to affect the pit of her stomach. She walked to the music box and lifted the lid and the music began to play. Maybe it was the weather that's it, she said out loud as she let the music soothe her. As she settled in for the storm tomorrow will be another day!

Chapter 9

It was mid-morning the following day as Nicky heard the conductor say Kearns next stop 15 mins as he gathered his stuff and prepared to leave. He was concerned about what Tila might be thinking of him; surely she showed up at the pond thinking he would be there. He knew how she felt! If not for the emergency of his mother. He would not leave without telling Tila what was going on. She was the closest thing to a best friend he had ever known if she was to not show he would feel sad. As he stepped off the train he headed through the familiar streets of his childhood down to wear the hospital that was built some many years back. AS he entered the doors he hurriedly made his way to the reception desk and asked for the number to his mother's room.

Then he made his way down the hall into her room as he entered his mother sitting up talking to the doctor. Hello! Mother! He said with obvious concern in his voice "Nicky my son" !!! she said not expecting to see him for he had been away since Christmas. mother i came as fast as I could I was able to catch the train last night. I am so pleased to see you and so swiftly I left as soon as I got your telegram. Yes my son I asked the doctor to send it because I was not sure what had happened to me or if I was going to be alright. What happened was that Nicky asked the doctor introduce himself and begin to explain "your mother while shopping blacked out and fell to the store floor. She was rushed here and we did some tests. Threw the result of those tests we have determined. She had a bad appendix so we had to do surgery last night and all went well. She should be fully recovered in a few days. Had we not caught it it could have been very bad for your mother reaching out and hugging his mother he felt tears run down his cheek.

I am so glad you are doing better. I am so glad you came to see my son. For the next couple of days Nicky stayed close to his mother doing whatever he could for the business and for her comfort. She was recovering quickly and already on her feet eager to go to work, all Nicky did in the time he had to himself was think of Tila. One day he had told his mother he had made a very special friend but he didn't mention she was a fairy. Still he missed her company and could hardly wait to get back to be around her. This was the second evening Tila sat at the rock where her and Nicky would meet at night. Last night she waited nearly all night long, falling to sleep because she was so overwhelmed with an empty feeling it was easier to sleep than it was to deal with the possibility that might exist, especially the idea that came from over thinking something to long.

Like Nicky might not want nothing to do with her which was worse than if he had disappeared off the face of the earth. Yet as she sat there on the rock she had a tear in her eyes and could not be idle any longer. She began to search for him. She followed the trail he had usually taken to the pond just as she did last night only this time she went beyond the forest. She had never gone this way beyond the trees never! She had gone beyond the forest in the direction of the setting moon for that was where the land of the fairies lie, and her mother her father had disappeared one day and had never been found or heard from.

Considering there are many dangers to a fairy it was hard to say what happened nonetheless it hurt and saddened her deeply. Has this happened to Nicky? No it was not possible. Maybe he had someone in the village, maybe there was an unforeseen reason for his disappearance. She had to look, she had become a very important part of his life and she was hurt and concerned which made a very painful combination of feelings. As she left the forest she headed to the lights of the village. As she came into the village she noticed there were a few humans standing around. She noticed buildings with lights and walls she could see through. She noticed inside of houses where people sat doing various things she was not sure of. She saw the humans laughing and playing. in one building she saw many men being very loud and drinking big glasses of yellow water with foam on it. There were some who were chasing women in bright colored covers and bright colored patches on their faces. But they were pretty and very tall. The covers they wore went from their necks to their ankles.

But would toss them high above their waists as they danced, But she did not see Nicky. She flew on going from window to window. She had not seen Nicky anywhere but she did notice a lot of men and women being and doing things together. Again she wondered if Nicky had someone like that. No she said out loud that thought was too painful. As she flew back to the forest she began to feel sad. But No Nicky! The hour was late and Tila found herself very tired! She seemed so drained and confused it made her just want to lay down. She could find no answers to her questions and as she entered her home she laid down exhausted and fell fast asleep.

It was the fourth day and Nicky had boarded the train late last night he was able to get the necessary things done to ensure all was well with his mother and his sister had shone up to work at the shop and to all the odds and ends that their mother could not do as of yet which was not much. She was a self- oriented woman. She had also seen and noticed the loneliness on Nicky's face being a mother she had that sixth sense for such things. But as Nicky looked out the window thinking of Tila he recalled his mother saying distinctively I wish to meet this Tila who had touched her son's heart so deeply which brought a blushing red to his facial appearance. He could just smile and think if mom only knew Tila was a fairy he began to wonder what Tila had thought of his disappearance unannounced and unexpected.

He hoped she was alright. He would be home just in time to go look for her. He said that his feelings for her were doom and that he had to consider telling her so but what could he do! They

38

were from different worlds and what did Tila know of the feelings he was coming to understand he felt for her. He had to speak with her. After all she was his best friend. half hour more he would be home the moon was already starting to light the horizon Tila was so exhausted she slept tell just about a hour before sunset when she woke she decided that she would make one more effort to find Nicky if she could not find him she would leave the forest and go be with her mother.

The evening was beginning to light up as the moon reached out upon the forest. She began looking at the edge of the forest where she knew Nicky would come from. As she searched in all directions she made her way to the pond. No Nicky, what could she do! maybe he did not want to see her any more. But how could that be possible? They had not argued; she began to check some of the places they had gone to. The berry patches the river she ran across Cheal, Huey and Brier but none had seen him. Brier said he would take a look around and meet her at the pond after a while. As she flew around she saw Jazmin and she had not seen him, what now she thought landing on a log next to a patch of flowers she lied her head in her hands and wept. The train was about to enter the station as Nicky prepared to depart eager to get home and to the forest as he left the station he ran down the street to his house unlocking the door he tossed his belonging into the door shutting it he ran past the buildings to the path that led into the woods.

Tila had met with Brier and no Nicky! Heartbroken, she went back to the cave and began to gather things up to go see her mother. Nicky stopped short of the woods to catch his breath, his lungs were burning and the heat was rushing to his head from running so hard. He had not noticed that he was pushing himself so he definitely had a strong desire to see Tila as he hurriedly trotted down the trail that led to the rock. He made it there in front of him was the rock as he approached it he began looking frantically around for Tila he did not see her he called out her name Tila! No sign of her and no answer he began walking around calling her name Tila. It's me Nicodemus are you out here somewhere Tila! He called! He began walking further into the forest Tila it is me Nicky! Still no answer, soon he saw Brier flying over- head Brier he called out but Brier just looked his way and continued to fly the berry patch yes he would check the berry patch. Calling her name all the way looking frantically he felt himself panicking Tila it's me Nicky please answer I had to leave are you out there?

Just then he saw a light there by the berry patch. Could it be Tila running to the light be called Tila I have found you I am sorry I had to leave but i couldn't help it my mother was sick as the light flew toward him he was showered with dust. Instantly he changed to a fairy. It was Tioga, it's me, Nicky Tioga. Oh Tioga have you seen Tila yes! My son, she spent many nights waiting for you and sadly she decided to go see her mother. You can check the cave but I believe she is gone! Before Tioga could say another word Nicky had flown away! At the entrance Nicky called out Tila! No answer. Tila it's me Nicky still no answer entering the cave he called again Tila are you here he was too late she was gone he sat as tears welled up in his eyes, saying I am too late!!!!

Chapter 10

Tila was standing on the ledge to Tioga house, when she turned she thought she heard her name! And it sounded like Nicky. As she listened she did not hear anything. Maybe it was that she wanted to hear it so badly, because she missed him so much. Now she was imagining things. She was so deep in thought she had forgotten that she had come to tell Tioga goodbye. Tioga it is me Tila are you in there. No answer she opened the door and stepped inside he was not to be seen. As she turned to go out she saw a note as she pulled it from the nail she read. "TILA WENT TO PICK BERRIES AND HERBS DID NOT WANT TO MISS YOU I WILL BE AT THE PATCH " Tioga. She smiled seeing that he knew she would come to find him and say good-bye after all they were like father and daughter: Tioga knew of her father and disappearance besides he never had any children and always wanted a daughter at least his wife and he had wanted a daughter but she had also disappeared a long time ago. Sometimes when a fairy feels it's their time they go off to some selected special place to expire as Tila replaced the note! She flew off to the berry patch to say good-bye to him As she reached the patch she saw Tioga right off. Mumbling as always she said Tioga I found your note! I knew you would, he said with a smile.

I have just come to say good-bye for I am not sure how long I will be gone. If you see Nicky by some chance would you let him know that I looked for him, and to tell him where I've gone. That is if he should ever come back to the forest! "Yes," Tioga said! I will tell him if you like but wouldn't you rather tell him yourself Oh yes I would like that but I have not seen him for days. I thought I told you! That oh you have my child but I happen to know that Nicky is at your house as we speak! WHAT! Tila said as she swore her heart skipped a couple of beat and she suddenly found it hard to breath yes he was just here I change him and he flew off to your place to try and catch you Tioga said as he turn to pick up he's bags in fact he said turning but there was no Tila. All he saw was the bags she was caring for and no sign of Tila.

He just smiled, grabbed her bags and headed home. He would drop them off to her later! Tila was not taking a chance of missing Nicky as she flew as fast as her wings would go! She kept calling his name all the way to her house as she entered where he was. Nicky!!! She said out loud running to him she hugged him as he jumped up and they both fell to the floor. I am so happy to see you Tila. I thought you were gone GONE! Speaking of gone Tila said as her expression changed dramatically and she took a solid stance in front of him. Do you realize I was there every night waiting not knowing where you were and what had happened to you. Whether you were hurt or not whether you didn't want to see me anymore or you had been with someone else, you didn' let me know a thing. I even went to the village looking for you but nothing. I felt like a part of me had vanished. You hurt me the tears welled up and she wept Nicky coming out of the shock of being glad to see.

Nicky understood how she might be feeling and the first time he had seen her mad, especially at him. And the shock of hearing her say she was concerned about him being with someone else which he took as hint of jealousy mixed his feeling of being apologetic, touch by her remark and confessing to himself about that he had affectionate feeling for Tila he was not sure he was ready to admit especially to her as Nicky took a step toward Tila he apologized for disappearing the way he did but that he could not help it his mother was sick very sick and he needed to be there. He also explained how he felt very bad about not being able to let her know for it happened so fast he told her that he missed her everyday she was gone and how he spoke of her to his mother and how he was so glad to see her. Tila wiped the tears from her eyes and embraced Nicky. I am sorry for being upset with you. It just came out. I am glad you are safe and glad you are here .

Tila caught herself as she was about to reply to the a with someone else" comment even though she was glad that he was not with someone else. But instead she replied. Or at least your mom is fine is she not? Oh yes she is much better. They released their embrace as two best friends would who just caught themselves in peculiar unexpected behavior. Could I offer you some food as Tila tried to change the atmosphere? Yes thank you Nicky replied eager to do the same as Nicky sat he had noticed how nice it was to look upon Tila. Tila brought a basket of berries and fruit next to where Nicky sat. She asked Nicky to tell her all about the trip to his mothers. So Nicky told her of the telegram and how he panicked and before he knew it he was on a train heading to his mother. He had to explain what a train was and he explained how they had to operate and what was involved with the recovery. Tila listened with interest when Nicky was through he asked Tila what she thought of going to the village?

Well she said I did see many things I did not understand. I saw men and women with their lips pressed together while they embraced yes that is called kissing! When two people are in love with each other they kiss. And she asked about the thing that floated on the endless lake. Micky explained that it was called an ocean and that those were boats that she saw he explained how they finished with them and traveled from place to place and sometimes just to float around he also told her how they used boats and rafts to float down the river on the rapids. She explained seeing the people in what she was told a tavern and the painted women. They talked on through the night Nicky explained many things to Tila that night about his world and some of the things that were available for recreation and activities of sights and sounds.

She listened content to have him near. As the hour grew late Nicky told Tila he must be going but he said he would be back tomorrow and he would never disappear again without telling her.

She was thankful for that and was glad he was back but sad he must leave. She will sleep at ease tonight. They said goodnight! With a hug Nicky went out the doorway saying I'll see you tomorrow with a smile she said tomorrow.

Chapter 11

As Nicky walked home again he recalled the hurt he was in Tila as she explained her searching for him and the loss she felt. He recalled her telling him about her father and how he had disappeared knowing now that him being gone brought that memory back to Tila. He was sorry because he knew that empty loneliness that comes with the loss or the perception of loss and the pain that comes with an overactive mind when trying to come up with answers for things unknown. Especially when it concerns the heart. He was fully aware of the concept of first concern I hope all is well! What could have happened? Were they alright, their loss! Is there someone else did they forget about me am I not important enough, the panic, what if their hurt? what if it's is someone else as in being replaced than the anger, pointing the finger the accusations the harsh unforgiving words) it takes something special to admit wrong and faults and even more to work threw them. Of course there was a relationship with some kind of foundation because he felt the emptiness in her absence.

He would feel the same if it had been reversed. Nicky felt for sure there was a foundation there already; she was definitely someone very special in his life. He was touched recalling her fragileness as she hid behind her anger, and her quick embrace that sent them both tumbling to the floor, reciprocating the joy of being together again. As Nicky entered the village he was glad to be back walking into the house. His bags on the floor one opened and scattered somewhat and smiled as he recalled his anticipating eagerness to get to the forest and see Tila. Picking up his belongings Nicky put them away then he crawled into bed looking forward to tomorrow and closed his eyes. Tila awoke in the afternoon glad to have slept with some comfort and peace at heart. As she began her day she recalled leaving her bags at the berry patch. She must go see Tioga and find out if by chance he had picked them up for her then she would have to clean her house. It had gone unattended the last couple of days and it was showing landing at Tioga's door. She caught him as he was coming out.

Tila my child he said I was just on my way to bring your bags. You went off in such a hurry yesterday and understandably so. Do come in if you like is all well? Oh yes Tila said all is well Nicky mother was ill and he had to leave suddenly. I hope she is well. Tioga said yes she is fine now. That is why he came back to my child! Tioga said I don't think that is the only reason he came back. Blushing Tila said he is human and I am a fairy. Okay Tioga said not wanting to force the issue. Would you like some tea? He asked yes I would thank you and they sat drinking tea and talking about the things of last night as Tioga listened patiently. Nicky awoke to the sound of children playing outside his window. As they laughed and squabble over a ball they were playing with he recalled his days at that age and how fun and non- stressful life was. Where the hardest decision was what you were going to do for fun. And who would be able to participate and what you were going to get for your Birthday or Christmas was the biggest anticipation of the year. Until school age that is. He did have a good childhood rolling out of bed. Nicky had an idea. He would go shopping but he would shop for things that he could take to Tila, things she might be able to use. Such as a chair or couch, a lamp or candle he was not sure what yet but he would see what he could find in the stores.

This he thought of well looking around his house at all he had remembering sitting on the rocks at Tila house. Maybe something soft like a blanket, maybe she wouldn't want them but he would find out. Besides, he could alway return the items. So he dressed and walked out the door. The first place he would go was the craft store. Entering the craft store he began to look around. There were so many things he did know where to start a couch? One they could both sit on? yea that would be a start. He felt kind of odd but he just wanted to buy something for her. It was a guy thing he thought as he smiled to himself as he looked around there were so many things that looked nice. Then he saw a couch. It was baby blue velvet with wooden arms and legs. There were two removable cushions. This was just what he hoped she would like. Then it hit him this was what he would like, but what if Tila did not maybe instead of getting a bunch of stuff he would get a couple of things and see how she liked them, he could always come back he also almost forgot about Tila having wings.

This was something he would definitely have to consider. And that couch would not work as he looked on. He saw a floor chest padded with a down cushion over the top like one to sit at the foot of the bed as a hope chest. It was very soft and it was made of red cedar which made it smell very good. That would work as he picked it up and put it in the basket he had. In one of the displays he saw a small oil lamp that was actually operable and whoever made it also made a funnel for filling it. He could put lamp oil in a small vial to refill it. I wonder if Tila is aware of fire. He doesn't recall it even being mentioned and whenever they had tea it was cold. He noticed that Tioga had a big black kettle that was under what looked to be a magnifying glass that would cause a source of heat. But no real fireplaces that he recalled except in the cave. Picking it up he figured that would be enough for now. He would go to the fabric store for some cloth for a blanket and some soft cloth.

After purchasing some of the softest cloth he could find and having it cut to the desired size Nicky decided he would walk out to the forest and see if he could find Tila. He had never tried going there during the day. After dropping off a couple bags at home he headed toward the trail that led to the forest. The day was very warm and there was a warm breeze that blew on his face. The grasshopper leaping from one side to the other with some flying off, as they made a clicking sound a couple of times he saw a lizard scurry off from a rock who was catching the midday sun. Reaching the forest he was aware of many birds busy flying from limb to limb and magpie chirping a distinctive warning call. A rabbit scurried to a pile of brush believing himself to be hidden as his tail stuck out. As he reached the rock a deer with one quick movement disappeared into the tree.

While bees and other flying insects buzzed from place to place. Reaching the rock he could not see the pond. He headed toward the waterfall to see if Tila would be there. The berry patch was alive with bees collecting pollen. It was obvious why Tioga collected them at night when these creatures were sleeping. That is the stream that must lead to the water fall so he followed it surely enough there it was certainly not as tall as he had known it being in fairy form but it was still beautiful he could clearly see the eagles nest upon the cliff. The eagle was probably off looking for food. Coming to the waterfall he called out Tila it's me Nicky are you home? Nicky!! She said what an unexpected pleasure! I must say I never expected to see you but am glad to. I thought I would bring you some things I bought thinking maybe you could use them. What did you get? Tila excitedly recalled the music box and necklace. Sitting by the river Tila joined him as he reached in the bag he had. First he pulled the chest out, setting it on the ground and making it as level as possible and solid. He told Tila it was for two people to sit together.

She walked over and sat on the chest. It was so soft she said as she found it very comfortable. When you are small you can sit with me, she said. But how will I get it into my house? That should be no problem. I should be able to get it inside the size I am, do you think so Tila said with excitement in her voice. Yes I believe it was a cave for humans a long time ago. Explaining in more detail. That would answer where the large objects came from and the coloring on the walls and the musky dark spot in the middle Tila, Nicky said that was a fireplace to keep the cave warm and to cook with. Fire! I have heard of this but never seen it said Tila then Nicky pulled out the lantern pulling some matches from his pocket he struck one the light the wick and replaced the glass cover. It began to glow. Tila looked on in amazement and rubbing her nose as the sulfur from the match stung her eyes as well as Tila flew into the cave Nicky worked his way inside getting a little wet but made it fine there was more than enough room. which surprised Tila she was shocked that he had so much room.

As he fixed the hope chest for her where she wanted it he showed her how it opened up to store stuff in. She was amazed there was so much room. She was also amazed that the lantern lit so much of the cave that she saw things she had never seen before and it made the air warm when she was close to it. Oh thank you Nicky I like everything thank you she again said as she smuggled into the cushion on the chest. You're very welcome said Nicky. I must get going Nicky said I will see you tonight. Just cover the top of the lantern to shut it off. Nicky had shown her how to use the matches he left and explained how she must be safe. you can meet me here Tila said if you like that is. Yes that would be fine Nicky said as he left the cave and out of the forest. He was glad she enjoyed the items he had bought and he would see her tonight.

Chapter 12

Nicky, not coming from a wealthy family had always been able to work hard, and at whatever job he did, he did well and to the best of his ability at the present he had two jobs one was stocking shelves at the local grocers and the other was cleaning up peoples yards. The money he made was more than enough to pay the bills and keep some away for whatever he desired. There was enough in his bank to hold him over for some time. The home he owned was given to him by his grandfather when he and wife decided it was time to travel the world while they had the opportunity. Last he heard they were overseas somewhere. Today he was going to stock shelves for the store that had received a new supply of merchandise. Nicky was eager to go to work because at the end of the day that he could clean up and go see Tila.

He was looking forward to some new adventures. It seemed like a very long time since he and Tila had done something adventurous besides he was beginning to enjoy the idea of flying it was becoming like some kind of hobby. Although the antenna things had not become accustomed to This skill he would try to utilize to the best of his ability. As odd as this arrangement was and might be to another person he had ever encountered, for some reason he did not see it as odd. Whether that was from experiencing it or for the fact he felt some attraction to Tila he could not be sure. It was time to To consider the fact that Tila had become very much a part of his life, not only by filling a void in his heart but becoming a continuing subject of his thoughts and concerns. It was time for him to go to work as he walked out the door. I will see you here tonight" Tila sang her own words to the melody of the music box as she pranced around the cave. Dancing to her shadow on the wall. She had spent some of the morning making images with the shadowy figure as she stood to one side or the other of the lantern. At first she was started because she had not noticed her shadow before and thought she was not alone. Which scared her somewhat considering the size and all. But now it was like a dance partner moving in rhythm and she tidy the place up knowing that Nicky would be showing up tonight she wanted the place to look nice hoping Nicky would appreciate it she had made several trips to merely flower patches picking the loveliest most fragrant one she could find, she straightened the blanket Nicky had given her that fit Nicely on her cotton bed. And rearranged the cat's paw pillows that she had. Looking around her she had accomplished quite a bit since she had been up. As she laid back on her bed she took a deep breath as the fragrance of the flowers began to fill the room.

She relaxed and closed her eyes glad to be experiencing the happiness she felt knowing Nicky was back and she would be able to take to the never ending lake or ocean as Nicky had called it. She tried to imagine a life existed on the other side for Nicky had told her of many lands afar. Other than home and looking for Nicky in the village the forest was the only place Tila had known she began coming here shortly after her father had disappeared as a means to escape the daily reminders of his absence; it was as if she had become irritated by things that had not mattered before.

A weight had suddenly been dropped on her and she wanted to get out from under it. So she took off one day and ended up in the forest where she was at peace and her mind was busy with other things like finding shelter and food. That is how she found the wise man. Since then she could not be without Tioga. He was like a father and that filled an empty space. Her mother did not necessarily like the idea but she knew Tila was a strong good minded child and was even more content to know Tioga lived in the same forest and was friends with Tila. Looking around Tila was pleased with the way her house looked and she soon fell asleep waiting for Nicky's arrival. As Nicky finished stocking the shelf. He had considered going to the craft store to buy a mirror for Tila that was something he thought she would enjoy since he had sister's in his family. He recalled the time they had spent in front of one and how hard it was to comb his hair sometimes or go to the bathroom. That brought a smile to his face as he left the store. As Nicky went to the counter the young lady inquired as to his recent purchase in the last couple of days. Nicky smiled and simply replied "my mother collects doll house items so I send them to her now and again."

He thanked her and headed home as he entered his house he saw the poster of the fairies he had purchased. Nicky wondered if any of it was anywhere near the facts of such a real place and if so how had the painter known was he the only one to see a fairy let alone speak with one or fly with one. Or heck even still! Be changed into one. He could not be the only one he would have to go to the library and see what kind of literature there was. It would be an interesting thing to do but for now the hour was getting late, he would take a quick nap before he went to the forest. He layed back pondering thoughts of Tila as he closed his eyes. Tila awoke eager with the idea of fixing a basket of stuff to eat and taking it to the ocean. While they look for stuff in the sand they could listen to the water and watch for stars falling from the sky. She gathers fruit and fresh water for she knew from experience that the water did not taste good when one tried to drink it she could not understand how the fish and other creatures could live in it.

She would also ask him why sometimes she would come across patches of rocks and they were all round and smooth, she enjoyed walking on them and it made her feet feel good. And she would ask him about the creatures she had seen on the sand. There were many things she would ask like the noise that came from nowhere periodically in the night and the light that would flash across the ocean. Yes she was eager for Nicky's arrival and it wouldn't be long now

Chapter 13

Nicky while walking through the forest had admired the moon. At its fullness things were well illuminated outlined with a transparent hue and a fluorescent glow. This would be an excellent night to do something. He had recalled when he met Tila it had been a half moon and that would always have a special meaning in his head. As he came upon the cave he called out. "Tila it's me Nicky" Hello she said! Are you ready for a fun night? Yes! I am what do you have in mind!! He asked if I thought maybe we could go to the ocean. I know a spot I like to go to that sounds like a wonderful idea, he replied! Close your eyes she said and before he knew it he was ready. Recalling all he had learned he moved his wings back and forth actually enjoying the feel of them. And the thought of the freedom of flight. Tilla came out with an arm full of stuff that Nicky offered to help with. She handed him a part of the load and off they went it took a few minutes to remember how to fly. Before he knew it he was comfortable and on his way as if he had never taken a break as they flew they had spotted Brier lightly landing on a rock perched high above an open field obviously hunting.

I wonder if he and Heuy are friends he thought to himself as they flew. Tila saw Jazmin stretching her long sleek body preparing for her nightly territorial responsibilities and to hunt food for her evening meal. Probably a rabbit or something like that. Nicky looked in awe as her size was overwhelming yet thought how majestic and proud she held herself. As they crossed the top of the rigid hillside that separated the forest from the ocean the scent of salt water was thick as the breeze blew somewhat stronger than in the forest. The moon glistened off the water gathered in pools of existing life, each one different from the other. Nicky led them down to the white sandy beach to a spot that where tide pools scattered separately throughout the shore line. The tall waves being damperd by the collection of rock compiled relinquishing the wrath of the waves beyond the shore. Here and there were flowers of many colors and ferns with long broad leaves and moss of all colors.

All clinging to the cracks and crevices of the cliff wall and adorned here and there by pines and ivy reaching and holding on to what life they could absorb from the wall's face. Tila chose her location and set down the basket she carried followed by Nicky. This is a very nice spot you have chosen Tila. We shall have a great time, yes and the moon is bright and beautiful. Let's go exploring said Nicky. Tila agreed and said follow me they took of some distance down shore and Tila came to a stop at a large tide pool where the ocean side of the rocks were covered with mussels and barnacles as the waves splash against the rocks it would emit a very thin misty spray of water about causing rainbows to roll across the mist. Nicky was looking out to the ocean as Tila called him. Come see there are many things in here as he looked in it was as if they were isolated from the ocean as a whole world content and undisturbed there were little fish some of which had to be baby cod at best as he could tell and Nicky began to explain some of what was there to Tila.

There were various shapes of coral forming at the bottom, starfish, orange, purple, red, some small, some very large. There were red rock crabs scurrying from crevice to crevice and clams that were open. Nicky had noticed that one had a pearl in it, as he explained the process of this creation he dove into the water forgetting about his wings. Thrashing about some he managed to get deep enough to pull a pearl out the size of a pencil eraser as he handed to Tila he said here is something for your chest I give to you! It is beautiful she said as she saw the color change when she turned it around in her hand she giggled at the display of Nicky fighting the wings to get into the water.

Nicky fanned his wings to toss what moisture he could from them and allowed the heat still captured in the sand from the day's sunlight to warm him dry. He continued to point out urchins, seaweed, and tube worms that were extended from their shells reaching to feed on the smallest of ocean life. The colors were so brilliant and fluorescent he pointed out the pinchers on the crabs and explained how they were a delicious meal when boiled in water. Tila seemed to shudder at the thought of being put in water the way he explained it. She had eaten fish before but she doesn't recall ever eating anything from the ocean. He explained that many things were used as food with the conversation at hand. They both felt hungry and headed back to the basket to eat some of what Tila had prepared.

As they enjoyed the various fruits vegetables and berries they watched out over the ocean the sounds were soothing and tranquil as they watched they saw dolphins and whales surfacing atop and out of the ocean they saw the whale as he sprayed from the blow hole atop his body and the fish that flew their short distance silhouetted against the moon. Nicky walked to the water's edge as he spotted a shell partially uncovered pulling it from the water he emptied it shaking it free of what moisture clung tight to it. Bringing it back to Tila he put it gently by her ear asking her to listen as she did he saw her eyes sparkle with amazement. He asked her if she could hear the ocean in the shell and she said yes I do! It sounds just like it! She said with excitement she began to ask him about the pebbles that were shiny and round Nicky explained the process. How constant tumbling of water and sand shaped and polished everything that collected in its repeating cycle.

Wood, rock, glass and shells after they had finished eating Nicky suggested walking down the beach together they walked kicking sand with their feet admiring the moon sparking off the sand. Tila pointed out the little creature that scurried back into the sand Nicky explained they were sand crabs. As they walked he caught a flash of light in the waves as he pointed out to the rising wave they saw the surf perch racing along the wave like they were playing tag back and forth as the moon reflected off their silver scales. He explained the fog and its purpose along with the lighthouse shining its light out to sea directing boats to safety. As they walked further down the beach they saw something moving slowly across the sand headed toward the ocean.

As Nicky looked closer he saw what it was! He said to Tila as he flew ahead with Tila right behind him as they approached the dark spot Nicky saw it was a very large sea turtle. Come on he said as he landed on top of the turtle is it safe Tila asked Oh ya he said it is a sea turtle, they don't move very fast on land but they are very quick and sleek in the ocean he told her how they very seldom came out of the water, mostly to lay eggs. Tila was flabbergasted to hear the rest of the process. Wow! Nicky thought out loud I could have never done this as a man. As the turtle headed to the sea they caught a shooting star flying across the sky disappearing. Jumping off the turtle they ran up the shore with a wave nipping at their heels giggling like school kids in a playground. The night continued with laughs and running down the beach flying around the waves and smelling and picking the flowers she would take home and dry. Flying back to the basket they gathered stuff they had collected and headed back to the cave. Upon reaching the cave they put things away.

Tila hung her flowers to dry, she placed the sea shell in a spot like a shelf in the rock wall, she would keep it and remember their trip to the ocean together. She could hear the sea among the stuff was drift wood and round polish rocks. Nicky lit the lantern as the room illuminated he had noticed the care she had put time into rearranging and the cleaning was done around the house and the vast spread throughout the house was filled with fresh picked flowers. As Nicky had an idea he began picking up pieces of wood and stacking them in the old fire pit. That had remained untouched for so many years. After filling the pit he gathered some larger pieces left scattered around the cave and stacked them on the side to burn later. Tila looked to ask him what he was doing! He said he would build a fire. A fire she said! Is it going to be safe? Oh yes! Said Nicky but I will start a small one so we will be safe for sure. As he started the fire Tila watched with marveled appreciation but concerned eyes. As the flames began to rise the cave was lit up even more than the lantern had allowed giving off much more heat.

The smoke found its way to the hole atop the cave traveling in a single cloud as Tila watched on. Twitching her nose a little as the smell of the fire mingled in the air. It was a warm cozy light and they both settled discussing the events of the evening as Nicky reached in his shirt pocket he had taken off before changing he pulled out the mirror for the size he was now it was almost full bodied. Tilas eyes lit up as they always did when he brought something new to her. That was a sight he could never get tired of. As she looked upon herself Nicky sat back and smiled. They relaxed on through the night which would end as always too soon!

Chapter 14

Nicky had left after Tila had fallen asleep. Some- time after she was asleep he couldn't help it but to just sit there and admire her beauty especially in the flickering fire light the waves of her hair flowed freely across the check of her face and down her slender shoulders her wings glistening in the light like a hundred twinkling stars, so vulnerable and still so self-sufficient he couldn't help but to wonder how she would look as a human female. Would it be possible if she still wanted to know him? he wondered. He could take her on a boat ride under the stars a night at the theater and a ride on a train. The new experiences would be endless. It had just dawned on him that he had not yet invited her to his house. He could fix dinner or something but he was not sure what she'd like. That was something he would have to ask her. She would probably enjoy the phonograph if he knew how much she enjoyed her music box. They could dance together, He could maybe bring the phonograph to the forest well, maybe not that would probably make people curious He had made sure the coals were low in the fire pit As he walked home he was realizing the endless journeys they could venture and explore. Then he also recalled his mother wanting to meet her. He wasn't sure how to deal with that situation yet. There were many more things to consider, than he was willing to evaluate at this time as he unlocked the door he went straight to his couch and fell fast asleep. Tila woke sometime shortly after Nicky left. She walked over and threw a couple pieces of wood on the fire as it smoldered and then was engulfed in flame. She found it pleasant as she recalled Nicky standing in the fire light his silhouette letting her know she was not alone. She enjoyed the heat that was apparent and the flames leaped up like mist in the morning running from the heat of the sun. Last night was wonderful. It was very enjoyable being at the ocean. She had become aware of many things she did not know and she had never been on a turtle before. She recalled him splashing in the tide pool. He struggled to get her the pearl as she recalled that she dug in her pouch and pulled out the pearl. It was very beautiful that she would put it in her music box. She was glad Nicky was a part of her life now and recalled how she was beginning to feel as she thought he would not come back.

He was certainly her best friend. She had never had someone she could go on adventures with and the only male fairies she had known were always too busy for fun. And they thought her an odd sort since she decided to wander off to the forest. It had not mattered to her for she had friends Tioga, Huey, Jazmin, Jason, Cheal, and Justin. She was also friends with the weasel but she had never caught his or her name. The weasel was always in too much of a hurry for other than hello! And good-bye and Brier of course to whom she had known the longest. But Nicky was able to be a part of her world as she was a part of his and that maybe filled a void she was unable to detect before. She too had wondered, especially after seeing the humans interact, wondered what it would be like to be a part of his world and see and experience things in a way that he has all his life. Will all that did was make her mind wonder more and more. She had been thankful to share her time with him and would look forward to much more time together. For now she would rest as she stared into the fire she faded fast asleep as the fire crackled with the burning of the coals.

Chapter 15

The time flew by like a summer rain. Tila and I have grown very fond of each other.

Here it was late summer and we have enjoyed each other's company. We have done some wondrous things together and there is no doubt that she is so much a part of my life that this is surely where my heart belongs. But what of the world that lies behind me it is so commonplace that I should not give it but a second thought my family which lives their lives so much differently than I that find satisfaction in material rewards and progression by the things that can't be taken with you in the end. I have surely come to ponder the things that we have to live with as humans, the so-called dominant creatures of this world but if I was to make that decision on my own I think not for when denomination is there so is destruction. Not only that the world we live in dictates our actual existence but is the structure of our mere being.

Whether it be of natural causes is not for our control for that we call an act of god. If so why the innocent, the ones who suffer for the most, well acts of man are considered the acts of all humans young and old. The animals have structure and a regard for tomorrow. Which is their world. a world in which one does not destroy but regulate with pure thought of tomorrow's benefits. Like a ruler of those in need we as humans pollute, torch, slaughter and disregard tomorrow's future for the selfishness of today's gain, yet we continue to populate in the name of family and union. Well as I ponder, my mind grows tired because I have had the opportunity to know a world where someone shares the simplest things in life and does not consider material things as wealth. And not of the heart.

Today as I meet with Tila we shall talk of things that we share and of the things we hope to experience and I shall only enjoy her company with every moment together for it is a treasure in itself. There are many adventures yet to experience and new experiences yet to venture. Tioga has made it possible that I am able to become a part of their world by eating a berry that exists at the base of the waterfall and today I will ask Tila if she would like to come visit my home. I have made all the arrangements necessary for us to listen to music There are only a few hours before sunset and I still get giddy knowing that I will soon see her. We have for the last week spent time learning of each other's worlds and of plants and such we talked of her home before the forest and it sounds like a pleasant dream conjured up by some storyteller who has experienced the realization of a world apart. She has offered to take me and I accepted. I shall meet her mother as she has yet to meet mine I have talked with Tioga and he said he would do what he could about making it possible for Tila t experience being human for a short while so she could share a part of the world I come from and have known all my life there are many things I wish for her to see and do that she could not do otherwise. I have come to know most of her friends and find them all very odd yet honest and good hearted creatures, the one I have not yet met actually two are Jason and Jazmin. Brier is very smart and Cheal and Huey argue with a love that is not much seen in a world like mine. I have spent time laughing so hard at their antics and Tila mother hens them yet they would be lost without each other.

Justin is a very well- mannered conversationalist, self- sufficient and one of the cleanest cautionary creatures in the world of this existence. I have seen the eagle a few times from my window in the village, circling the forest like a guardian angel large and majestic with no equal in the air. I have heard of Toiga being able to converse with the dominant King of the sky but have never inquired farther. As I finish up some last touches in the house I will prepare the fireplace knowing Tila enjoys it so much. I hope I have not forgotten anything I shall leave in a moment. It is a warm beautiful night entering the forest. Nicky was startled by a sound loud like a crying baby as he stepped forward leaping before him was a large cat.

Eyes orange like a flame, teeth large and white there was obvious aggression in its demeanor but Nicky thought that this might be Jazmin. He began to speak low and gentle but there was no response as he tried to raise his hand the cat crouched and growled low in its throat a warning he was sure he tried stepping backwards and that seem to only infuriate the cat even more so Nicky was worried for now he did not believe this to be Jazmin and if it was how was she to know that he was Tilas friend for they had never meet nor had she seen them together before. He was not sure what to do now but he was sure he was not safe. Nicky had not shown up as Tila waited for him although it had not been that long she was also eager to see him. I'll go meet him on the trail she said to herself as she flew off the rock into the woods. The trail was still dark for the moon had not come up high in the sky as of yet so it was hard to actually see what the dark spot that was there before her as she saw Nicky standing very still, as she begin calling out his name she stopped half way through noticing that it was a big puma crouched ready to lung at him Nicky began to look up and Tila saw the muscles tighten in the hind end of the cat she was not able to help.

Nicky saw the cat as it began to leap from the ground directly toward his face. He saw the claws extended long and sharp and the teeth that seemed to grow as the mouth opened to rip at his skin. Farther up and forward the cat came completely off the ground, its eyes were aglow with anger as drool left the side of its deadly jaws. Nicky could feel the heat from its mouth as its left claw swiped for his head the right claw begin to puncture the side of his shoulder he tried to drop to the ground to avoid obvious disaster it was too late as he closed his eyes he heard Tila screaming loud frightened the scream was deafening. The cat startled pulled its paws back just a little but it was enough for Nicky to make it to the ground and began to roll to one side grabbing a tree branch to try and protect himself but he would not make it up in time for the cat had hit the ground spun around and was leaping for the final blows as Nicky covered his face with his arms.

With a hollow thud there was a moment that seemed to stand still. The fear was so bad that he could not feel the claws and teeth ripping at his flesh; he hoped his death would be sudden as he called out to Tila. Who was screaming his name. Again! he heard a thud and the sound of cracking branches as they snapped then he heard loud hissing growling and what sounded like deafening screams Tila brought him back from his confusion as she grabbed him pulling him back he was able to see what had happened there in front of him were two cats rolling under the trees blood and fur flying through the air as claws and fangs dug deep into flesh. It's Jazmin Tila said holding ever so tightly to Nicky.

As quick as it had started it was over as Jazmin chased after the rogue cat expressing her dominance and passion of her territory as the cats disappeared in the darkness of the forest with only the cries of victory in the wind. Nicky was up unharmed except for a scratch from rolling on the ground and a bruise or two he and Tila headed toward the pond so Nicky could wash himself off a little and them would head to the cave as Nicky was washing he saw the cat his muscles tense than he heard the words are you okay? Tila called Jazmin's name out loud and answered yes we are fine and Nicky is safe thanks to you. Otherwise he would not be here right now. Jazmin this is Nicky he said thank you for saving my life. I thought for sure I was a goner. I had never seen that cat before Jazmin said but I assure you he will never come around here again! I must be going as she headed off through the shrubs. Nicky called after her thank you Jazmin your welcome he heard her say. As he turned to face Tila, are you going to be alright she asked him. I am a little shaken but I should be fine. Would you like to go to the cave she asked? Well he said I was kind of hoping you would like to go to my house if you don't mind! Yes that would be fine she said to Nicky as he stood he told Tila to hang on as she sat on his shoulder they headed to the village.

Chapter 16

How did you know I asked Tila, I was making some early rounds when I heard you scream! So I came running. I am glad that I was in time to help. So this is Nicky. Hello I have heard about you from Tila. If I can help again don't hesitate to call! As they entered the village it was not quite dawn so there was hardly anyone up and about there were a few lights on, for the fisherman that would head out to sea to do some fishing and a restaurant that was preparing for the breakfast rush.

Tila held close to Nicky as they came to his house he unlocked the door and they both entered Tilas eyes were those of a child's which had just looked upon the largest playroom they had ever dreamed of. Even though she did not know what many of the items were she was marveled to see so much. The crystal caught her eyes as it reflected the light in the room. She flew over to the couch and landed. Nicky went to the fireplace as he lit it the room glowed with flickering light as it slowly began to heat up then he went to the phonograph and turned it on as the music began to play Tila flew over and landed on the edge of the table. Is that a music box she asked no said Nicky it is called a phonograph it plays music off the disc called albums.

There are many different kinds as there are music. Tila began to sway her head to the sweet sound that was captured by her ears. She asked Nicky if he would like to be changed. He said yes but wanted to prepare a few things first. Tila began to fly about the room as

Nicky took care of a few last minute items. Going to the fireplace he added a few more pieces of wood that would burn for a good long time. He placed the water pot next to the flames so he could prepare some tea. Then after laying out some food which consisted of crackers, cheese, chips, clams, oysters salad and fruits he turned to Tila saying I am ready! She smiled and as she tried she was unable to change Nicky she could not understand. Maybe it is the place where we are, it is not the forest and the magic may not be here so she said the special words and it was so. Nicky had changed and he flew up next to Tila with a smile on his face as he asked Tila if she would like some hot tea.

I would enjoy some thank you! Nicky had prepared some tea in a small tea set he had bought at the craft store. He poured the tea and handed her a cup. How are you feeling/? She asked if I am very sore but I am thankful for Jazmin if she had not shown up when she did. I dare not think of what the outcome would have been. I share the same feelings she told him. She could see his cuts would heal fine, still she pulled a plant from her bag which would help the healing. She rubbed it in the palms of her hands until the moisture was a visible paste. Then she put it on her finger and massaged it onto the cuts and visible bruises. It was soothing, Nicky noticed as she applied it ever so gently. Her touch alone was soothing as he closed his eyes and stored the moment in his mind to recall at times when she was away. Are you okay she asked? Oh yes! He said not noticing she had quit applying the medicine. I was very scared, she said! Looking into his eyes I was so helpless.

I could not move. Are you going to be okay he asked? I should be, I am still somewhat shaken now that I recall the moment. I think tonight would be a good night to just relax by the fire and listen to the music and if you feel like it you can show me what some of this stuff in in your house is Tila said relieving any pressure he might have about being obligated to other than a slumber night the fire was warm and soothing as the steam from the pot drifted up and vanished as they drank there tea they ate some piece of cake Nicky had prepared. Tila enjoyed it because she had never had such food before. The Tea was warm as it went down and had a slight hint of apple with spice. Tila began to inquire of the items about the house. It was not a surprise to Nicky that the simplest of items were intriguing things, we take so much for granted. The solitude of a clock as it ticks away the house, the serenity of a crackling fire, the detail engraved in an item made by hand, the sharing of a soul as it's portrayed in a portrait or a painting.

A flower's fragrance as it emits its last breath of like such things are past beyond thought because of desires to succeed materially in a world of inevitable pressures and dilemmas. Yet here I sit content sharing what has become the least of my concerns with an individual that I contemplate giving it all up for just to share her friendship In a world less demanding. as Tila goes to the shelf above the fireplace she inquires about the woman who is by Nicky's side in a block of wood. He averts his eyes as she returns to his side. How did you come to be on a block of wood? Nicky explains that is a picture the photographer turns it into a picture like you see. The wood around it is a frame. All those are pictures someone drew, painted or photographed. As he pointed to the walls. Tila flew from wall to wall admiring what she saw. Then back to the photo on the fireplace. It was obvious to Nicky he would have to explain.

She said that the woman is beautiful. She has long wavy hair, bright blue eyes and a very nice smile on a soft beautiful face. Who is she? Tila asked again. Nicky began to speak paused and continued her name was Jolene did she change her name Tila asked no he said she was lost in the ocean. Lost? Yes! she was going to come and be my wife from a far-away place but, the shipwrecked and no one survived. Oh! Tila said suddenly ashamed to have asked I'm sorry. Nothing could be done. He said no one made it. What do you mean by marry? I was in love with her? Love! Caring more for her than anyone, my best friend in the world, someone to laugh and play with who made me smile and feel good. I see she said it must have really hurt, yes it did he said it was how you might have felt when your father was lost. I certainly do understand, she said.

Relinquishing to the silences of the contemplation of loss. Not wanting to push an obvious sensitive situation Tila looked around then she saw it wow! Wanting to change the subject she said as she flew toward the picture on the wall she landed on the bed! What is this she asked with a curious excitement? It is a picture I bought at the store Nicky explained. I was wondering if it was similar at all to anything you knew of but mostly I keep it where I can be reminded of us flying around together. That is kind Tila said although it's not like where I come from I am sure this can be considered just as beautiful. They continued to talk of the many things Tila could see and was serious about and it was getting late and it had been a very adventurous eventful day. They went back to the couch sitting in front of the fireplace and relaxed as the fire flickered and crackled they shared its heat. Tila laid her head on Nicky's shoulders and as she looked again to the picture on the fireplace she told him how thankful she was that he was okay and that she had enjoyed this time at his house very much.

Nicky closing his eyes heard Tila say I wonder what it would be like to be a human as she closes her eyes. Tila awoke somewhat startled as a flicker of light caught her eyes as she looked she saw the sun reflecting off the round thing in front of the window below her was Nicky he was himself again and she was on his chest he looked so innocent laying there sound asleep even at his size. She watch as he sleep reaching out she touched his face and then put her hand to his lips she could feel the warm breath come from within he made her happy, and she wondered again as she looked at Jolene and him in the picture she reached up and put her mouth to his cheek kissed him and said I am glad I met you Nicky as she placed a flower on the table and flew back to the forest.

Chapter 17

On the way home the air was crisp and fresh as Tila enjoyed the warmth of the sun as it peaked over the mountain to a new day. What a very beautiful day as the morning sky was embarrassed in bright purple, orange and red tinted with a blue haze as the night gave way. She was filled with joy that she had a very wonderful time with Nicky. There were many things she had learned and seen she may never have if not for him, especially this feeling in her heart that he filled so well. How comfortable it was to lay her head on his shoulder and feel safe and content. That is how she felt any time he was near she thought about the place that she came from. It was a most beautiful place as was the wall picture that was at Nicky's house. Here was that of some untarnished land where all was compatible and destruction was the mere picking of plants, berries, and fruit when one did not have the need for them. There was an atmosphere that was unhampered by the world outside although there were no walls it was certainly a world apart.

High above a very steep and very jagged mountain above the clouds it was a castle made of silk adorned with the rays of sunlight which illuminated at night like the northern star. Everything around the castle was beautiful: the flowers, the mushrooms, the plants and trees. All of which were homes or shelters for the desire. The weather was always warm and the sky always blue. There were no skies like the one before Tila at this moment nor were there sunsets as beautiful as ones that reach a deep purple as it is engulfed by the sea and put to rest. But there are many things that cannot compare to the world she now lives in the forest. She would not want to live anywhere else. As she made it home she sat below the falls to watch the sun rise up and reach into the forest with probing rays of light. Listening to the birds as they sang merry melodies to greet the day and scurry to and fro beginning the tasks of foraging for food and objects to build or secure their nests before fall set in.

Nearby Tila heard the chirping of a nest of baby birds as their mother set out on the never ending chore to feed their hungry little mouths. A small lizard crawled up on a rock anticipating the rays of sunshine that would embrace him and a chipmunk scurried down a tree chattering with a sense of caution and eagerness. Yes it was truly a beautiful day. As Tila flew inside she wound up the music box and sat down on the soft bed enjoying the sound of music as she recalled the music at Nicky's house it was so much different and so soothing. As was her music box but it was certainly different she was thinking how much different she felt away from him as opposed to being with him. She recalled the photograph above the fireplace. How happy Nicky looked as did Jolene. They looked very nice together. She was beautiful, her hair was so wavy and long and her smile glistened. They certainly looked to be in love as Nicky had said. She was very sorry for his loss and at the same time couldn't help but to evaluate her feelings for him.

She was very much pleased by his attention and the way she felt when they were together was like no feeling she had ever felt before. She made him smile and laugh showing she was happy and they had fun together. She was sad and empty when he had not come around for those few days that seem to last forever. He was most certainly her closest friend; they enjoyed each other's company. He was the most gorgeous man she knew or male for that matter and when he was attacked she had never felt as scared or frightened in her life even more so than the spider. She could have used some magic powder then but they were saved by Brier just before she was going to toss it out of her hand. There was no magic for the puma she could do nothing but picture him as defenseless he certainly took up a good deal of heart time and was always a subject of her thoughts and very much a part of her heart. She could not be sure because she did not quite know what it was.

She knew the feelings but was more involved she had never heard of a fairy being human. It would be nice to find out she thought as she contemplated the idea. She recalled seeing the ladies with paint on their faces kissing the men and hugging them as they sat on their laps obviously enjoying themselves for they laugh and smile. She recalled the other things she saw as she looked from house to house looking for Nicky, even the small children happy as their mothers played with them. She was sure she would very much like to experiencing Nicky's world as a human but she could maybe only wonder of course she could check with Tioga and see if anything was possible and it couldn't hurt to ask. She would make it a point to speak with him this afternoon when she knew he would be awake.

For now she would tidy up some and take some time to pick some fresh flowers to replace the old ones which she'll have to dry as the thought crossed her mind she recalled the flower she left for Nicky and wondered if he would notice she stood there also in recollection of the touch of his face and kissing of his check how soft his skin was on her lips and he smelled in a way that brought bumps on her skin. I wonder if she thought about how he feels about me. Does he enjoy being with me as I do him? Would she enjoy doing things in his world as he seems to in hers? She had to paint her face and dress like the women she saw. They looked like they would be confined and uncomfortable yet they were smiling and enjoying themselves. Yes she would get ahold of Tioga he would certainly have the answers. It was time for her to pick some flowers as she flew to her favorite patch she saw Jason walking down a small trail he had worn between his house which was in a very remote spot and a small cavern in the side of the hill where he would dig out shiny gold rocks he would use to make things with.

Jason was an elf. Just a little shorter than she was and built muscular as one would be who worked very hard and carried heavy items. His hair was dark wavy and always kept short. He wore his clothes loosely and his pants bagged down from his hips. He wore shoes made of some wood he had shaped to fit his feet. And a hat made from a leaf that kept the sun off his face which was wrinkled from the weather and a look of wisdom he was well known to all who communicated with him as one who could fix things and create things to accommodate one's needs. He was a very kind soft spoken elf. Tila called out to him hello Jason! Hi Tila! He said in a kind voice how are you on this fine day. I am fine. How are you? She said I am a very busy elf these days. I am trying to invent a way to reflect the sun into my home to use as a light and heat source.

So I have to gather some reflective material. I have yet to come up with the proper chemicals to create a material that will do what I need. I discovered it as I stood by the pond and the sun bounced off the water and I felt the heat. Marvelous isn't it. It sounds wonderful, she said, not really? I must be on my way, have a good day! You too he said as he scurried down the trail Tila giggled to herself as she flew away. Coming to her flower patch she began picking and smelling the flowers. These will look very nice she said out loud as she filled her arms and headed home.

Chapter 18

Nicky woke quickly as he looked about his house, not leaving the couch, but Tila was nowhere to be seen. The fire had died out and a few coals burned brightly glowing against the red brick. As Nicky laid his head down he saw the flower she had left a wide smile touching his face. Picking it up he laid it on his pillow looking up at the picture of himself and Jolene Recalling the very questions that Tila had asked. He missed her very much as he felt the emptiness in him because of his loss of her. It was the first time in a while he had been reminded of the pain that haunted him since her heartbreaking death. Laying there he began to remember the first time he had ever seen her. He was with his mom back home. They had gone to the grocery store to pick up a few things for their supper.

As they wandered through the store Nicodemus came around an Isle and collided with Jolene who was stacking shelves with groceries that had just been bought to replace that which was sold. After apologizing and being sure she was alright he introduced himself after a few unnecessary visits to the store he had found out that she was visiting an Aunt and Uncle who owned the store. She was from the village where he now lived. He was so fascinated by her beauty he found it hard to say anything when he was around her. As they got to know one another she was staying for a couple of months. He had brought her flowers a couple of times and finally asked her out. They went and had a very nice dinner together. There last night together they made arrangements to write. As they sat under a beautiful star lite night they had shared a very special couple of months together biking, picnicking, swimming and many other activities when Jolene had leaned toward him to say goodnight he kissed her lips and they held each other close as they begin to regret the dawning of a new day.

Jolene said she would be back when she found her father as they had promised before her leaving they wrote to each other when she got there. Nicky had purposed 6 months later she had wrote Nicky about her luck in finding him and would be home soon when he went to the dock hoping she would show up he was very sad to hear that the ship had sunk. Thus eventually going to the woods of and on just to escape from the pain and anger he felt for he could hardly believe it to be true. Nicodemus chose the forest as his escape. There he would sit in silence wondering why she had to be taken when she was he would recall the laughter and the tears of joy. The warmth of her embrace as her skin touched his. The plan to raise a family the smell of her perfume and the way her hair would shine as the sun silhouetted her frame. Her laughter was as musical as her voice was. The fragility of her innocence as she would lay asleep with her world content. Yes he certainly missed her as he came to know Tila he saw qualities equal to Jolene and found some peace from the pain. Tila! Does make me feel many of the same ways he thought as he shook his head. What a predicament.

How real was his feelings, although he was not sure, somethings speak for themselves as he put his hand near the flower smelling its fragrance as he closed his eyes wanting to get more sleep. For he was very tired Cheal was tuning circles as he searched irritably for Huey. Huey leaped from the stump near Cheal landing on his back yelling! "gotcha fur ball" as he leaped to the ground hiding in some tall grass nearby as Cheal spun around taunting heavy rat! Here rat! He called out as he dug at the pile of leaves as leaves were being flung every way Huey ran through the falling leaves were being flung every way Huey ran through the falling leaves diving for the hole in the rock just as Cheal swapped eagerly toward Huey. cheal having about enough of the tomfoolery it's about night time Cheal said as he lay on the ground taking a deep breath. Huey slowly worked his way to Cheal, being cautious as to make sure it was not a trick. They cuddled next to each other as they always did when it was time to close their eyes to sleep! As Tila came to the entrance of the cave she heard Tioga arguing with himself.

She flew into the entrance, laid the flowers down and headed off towards Tioga. He was busy collecting leaves from various plants about where he stood. There were some he had begun to collect using a piece of wood to knock them off the plant and scoop them onto a bag. Hello Tila it is good to see you he said not looking up for he was being very cautious as to the handling of his newly picked leaves. Tila smiled and asked him why he was carefully using a sickle. Tioga explained the leaf had little tiny needles on them that would sting and cause numbness. And make the skin swell if not handled carefully. After accomplishing the task he turned to her with a big smile and said it is good to see you my Child. I had noticed you had not come home last night. Did you and Nicky have a good time? Oh yes she said! We went to his house in the village.

He showed me many things that were new and wonderful. He showed me a music box that was called a phonograph. He showed me images of people called photographs and he showed me different kinds of food. Like sea fish, breads, and cheeses, some were really wonderful. We watched a fire in his fireplace. He showed me a crystal that caused the sun to reflect different colors on the walls. I really had a good time, she said with a smile on her face.

I see you did he replied to Tioga I was wondering as she paused, Tioga asked seriously! What is it my child? I've been wondering she started again! Well I was wanting to know if a fairy had ever been or I meant wanted to become human? Not shocked at all as she expected him to be. He rubbed his chin and began to rub his hand over the top of his cane which he did when he was looking for the course of which to explain something or speak seriously. It is not surprising that you would ask he began. Noticing the sudden surprise on Tilas face she had the look as if to inquire but chose not to. I was approached already on this matter. Nicky? She asked. Yes, it was him!

Just not too long ago. And I have done some research and inquired here and there and "Yes," she said with eagerness. And I believe I can come up with a special magic that can make this possible if all goes well. As a matter of fact these leaves I have been gathering are very much a part of the ingredients I will need. Along with some good fortune for it is a magic that has not been used for many centuries Excited, Tila asked if there was anything she could do to help for she was beginning to believe it might be something she would like to try! Nicky had already asked. So he had considered this for them to be together as humans then she recalled something about him saying his mother wanted to meet her. She would love to dance and go on a train. Sail on a boat and walk the beach together and go to the stores Nicky had spoke of all the wonderful things they have to offer. Yes, she could enjoy it very much. Upon helping Tioga she asked if there was anything else she could do to help. He laughed and said he could handle the rest. See ya later she said as she flew off to get something done and get some rest.

Chapter 19

Her first visit was as he had anticipated Tila seemed to have a very good time learning new things and the experiences that went with them. He enjoyed her company and was concerned whether she had a good time or not. As he laid there on the couch letting his eyes adjust to the awakening moment he would have to talk with Tioga about him asking if it would be possible for Tila to become human for a little while to share in his word if It was possible what he would like to do! Waking, he prepared to go for a walk to the forest and see if he could locate Tioga.

Certainly he must know something. A short time had passed as he was walking into the forest. As he passed the rock to the path that led to the falls Nicky said the plant that had the berries that had first turned him into a fairy as he plucked the berry the bush vanished as before eating the berry he recognized the change and should have transformed. Hearing a noise he turned to see Justin the racoon going through a berry patch he had come across in his feeding escapades. Hello, he said. Hello! Was Justin's reply how are you? Nicky asked as he introduced himself. "Oh" Justin said! Yes you are Tilas friend I saw you on the river once. Yes you did Nicky replied I am going to speak with Tioga is he about? I am not sure, said Justin but you might check up there as Justin pointed skyward.

Thank you Nicky said as he flew off Justin said nice to meet you and wandered off. As Nicky reached Tiogas house he hollered out and he was soon answered as the door was opened. Nicky! How are you, please come in, Tioga said, looking to see if Tila was with him, have a seat. Nicky if you like I was just working on what it is you came to inquire about. How did you know Nicky asked well he said it seems to be the subject of conversation today. Somewhat puzzled, Nicky said I'm not sure I understand Tioga, well I was speaking with Tila about this earlier. She seemed quite inthusiastic about the possibilities of her being able to be human for a period of time.

She seems to be quite fond of you Nicky and you must understand that there is so much responsibility involved Tilas life is purely in your hands and so are the choices you make together if harm should befall her it is the same as if it were here. Whereas here some things can be taken care of by my magic but not as a human. You must understand this as must she. In Fact I think it is important that we get together and discuss this fully together before any choices are made. Yes I agree, said Nicky. I shall go and see if she would like to do this and is really willing to go through with this. Nicky said as he headed for the door. She should be at home Tioga said as Nicky went out the door.

I will go and see if she is as Nicky made his way to Tilas place his mind seems to be going in many different directions. There was the joy in being able to share his world with her in his human level all the experiences they could share. Then there was the concern of any possibility something could go wrong. He surely would never want any harm to come to Tila for he was very aware of his feelings for her. There was also the curiosity of how she would look as a human female. What kind of change would occur as a result of whatever it was she would have to go through. Also what about the transformations back how long was it going to last? Would there be side effects? So many things he thought as he entered the opening to Tilas house. Tila! Tila, it's me Nicky are you here? Yes! Please come in, she replied I was just wanting to get ahold of you and here you are! I had gone to speak with Tioga and he said you might be at home.

We talked about the possibilities of being able to change into human and spend some time in my world. Yes, said Tila. I too had spoken with him earlier about that very same thing! Nicky said that Tioga had mentioned all three of them getting together and discussing the matter. She agreed Tila! Nicky said I do not want anything to happen to you! I care very much about you! As I do you said Tila and we shall view every aspect before I choose whether or not this is something I will follow through with or not. Good said Nicky we shall get with Tioga. Excuse me, Tila said there are a few things I would like to finish up here before we go. I shall be done shortly, said Tila. As Tila was busy around the house Nicky began to ponder! As he recalled his first encounter with Tila a smile began to cover his facial features as he blushed somewhat at his awkwardness that may have caused embarrassment for him he recalled the rafting trip the spider web and the wonderful time at his house where it left so natural to be content with the world.

He recalled wandering into the forest heartbroken at the loss of his loved one, how empty he felt and how he just wanted to get far far away. He recalled the encounter with the wild cat that almost brought him his demise and how grateful he was that Jazmin saved his life. He recalled Tila laying silent fast asleep and how his heart changed beats and butterflies tickled his belly as he looked upon her beauty and how the moonlight enhanced the sparkle of her eyes and made her hair glow. Excitement seemed to grip him as he thought of how it would be to hold her as a human would her laugh still be like a melody? Nicky! Nicky! Returning from his apparent daze he could hear his name as he looked up to see Tila are you all right she asked! Oh yes he replied my mind was just wondering shall we go she said! Yes I'm ready Nicky said! As they went out the opening of the cave Tila was looking at Nicky somewhat quizzical obviously trying to decipher Nicky's thoughts!

He just smiled and off they went! As they reached Tioga's house he was there, opening the door! Come on in he mumbled as he was busy thumbing through a large thick book that looked to be made of large leafs and tree bark for a cover. Please make yourself at home. I shall only be a minute more. Nicky and Tila sat down at the table where there was hot water for tea and a bowl of fruits and berries. As they sat there drinking tea they watched Tioga scurry back and forth grabbing small jars that had to have the dust blown off them so the label could be read. He would put a pinch of this and a pinch of that into a crystal bowl mixing and grinding as he went. He would stop momentarily only to read from the large book, make a few "a huh yes a huh" noise and continue to create his potion. Yep that should just about do it!

Tioga said with a smile on his face as he turned the curious look on Nicky and Tilas face was priceless he chuckled don't worry I believe it will be alright as long as she doesn't turn into a fish or a tree! He said teasingly they both looked at each other and began to chuckle. Tioga sat down and poured himself a cup of tea and he began! Let me tell you a story from days of old. In the beginning we the fairies were created to be caretakers of the world to keep balance and harmony in the world. We could interact with most any kind of life humans included. Yet as time passed people began to change they became greatly selfish and destructive they became hurtful and we could no longer interact. We soon became invisible to the bigger part of the human race. Yes there were those who still believed in what we believed and that was good but as people changed more we soon found only a small handful of people we could trust.

So it is today! Yet as time passed those fairies who had been influenced by the bad habits of the humans such as the destruction of plants and animals and who were chaotic and spiteful were turned to humans to live in the world they chose forever. That is something that is still a part of our world to those who do not follow the way we live. Eventually there were those who were wise and wanted to make sure what they were doing was right! So they came up with this potion I have made here! It allowed them to be human to interact in that world for knowledge. They would be able to transform themselves three times and three times only, but! The third time was indefinite and there was no turning back! And upon the third time they would forget all knowledge of fairy land completely! So you see there are risks such as if something should happen while you are human you will have to deal with it on those terms.

If you should have the need you have but to say "fairy sight and fairy mind. Fairy and human be untwined" and you will immediately be returned to as you are now. Should you choose to do this I will give you enough for three transformations but you must remember the third one is indefinite. Upon saying that he laid a vile made of an oak tree branch on the table inside this vile are three tablets all you have to do is swallow and recite these words and you will change. "Essence of herbs, twinkling dust by the power of potions do what you must days of old when worlds entwined change the body but not the mind from fairy to human before my eyes my choices are few with only three tries" That is all you'll have to do and you'll change is there any questions he asked there was silence then Tila said soberly no Tioga I've understood all you've said.

Good was Tioga's reply. Please, you must be very careful. I will worry very much about you! You are like a daughter to me. You must be safe and know I am here for you always, he said somewhat drawn and teary. Tila reached for his hand and said you are like a father to me and I will always hold that in my heart. I will be safe, Nicky not knowing what to say just sat there quiet as he watched the love that was between Tila and Tioga well it seems to me Tioga said you children have a choice to make. Be safe and good luck thank you Nicky managed to get out somewhat reserved yet thankful for the opportunity at hand. Yes thank you Tila said as she gripped Tioga in a hug that about made him stagger her face was aglow and he could sense the eager joy in her tone! Good luck and be safe he said in her ear. Tila looked at Nicky and curiously asked are you ready? If you are all Nicky could respond with good luck Tioga said as they flew off headed to Tilas house as they reached the cave Tila full of smiles and excitement began to tell Nicky how anxious she was to get started as her mind raced through so many scenarios she would like to explore. Nicky could only smile with concern and excited feelings of his own. Oh yes she replied right away! inside the cave Tila began to look around as if she were to pack for a trip but could not figure out what she could possibly take seeing's how she would no longer be small panic started to grab her as Nicky noticing said it will be alright there are somethings at my house that you will need and could use! The rest will have to get. Does that mean I can go shopping? Yes Nicky said with a grin you can go shopping! Will go together. Maybe we should go to my place so that way you'll have clothes to wear. That sounds fine to me Tila said with eager anticipation Nicky began to realize how vulnerable Tila will be at first but knew she was strong-willed with good judgment and definitely very smart. Shall we go? Tila said! Yes we shall reply to Nicky and off under a bright half- moon the flew into the night.

Chapter 20

Entering his house Nicky began to feel a rush of energy, a feeling of wholesomeness like he had never felt before. He too was eager to be able to share so many things with Tila he could not decide what he would like to do first. Tila began to tell Nicky how ready she was and Nicky reached for her hand looking her in the eyes and asked her! Are you very sure you want to do this? Yes Nicky I am as sure as you were when you were willing to change to spend time with me. Okay he said as Tila released his hand backed away removing the vile from her pouch she removed one pill set it on her tongue and swallowed Essence of herbs twinkling dust by the power of potions do what you must. Days of old when worlds in-twined change the body but not the mind from fairy to human before my eyes my choices are few with only three tries. As they stood there with reservations about the situation began to fester and just as Nicky was about to say something Tila said she felt dizzy and fell to the floor. Nicky picked her up and set her small form on the bed. Tila grabbed her stomach and brought her knees close to her chest with fear in her eyes Nicky began to panic. Is there anything I can do? He would ask anything at all.

There was no reply. She would just lay there and stare, bundling herself into a ball Nicky ran to the faucet to get some water and as he turned there before him was a full grown woman semi curled up. He stood there, mouth opened as he saw Tila begin to realize the change. Looking at herself with total amazement and awe! She began to sit up realizing she was not wearing a thing she grabbed the blanket and put it around herself. Are you alright? `` she said finally looking at Nicky. Nicky just stood there and traced in his mind the astonishing beauty that was before him. Nicky are you all right she said again more concerned than before. Shaking his head he said yes! Yes! I am fine I was just well I was a my you are so beautiful, I'm sorry I just wow! Nicky! Oh yes some clothes he said out loud to himself he turned to go to the closet but could not keep from looking back as he almost ran into the closet door. Reaching inside he pulled out a suitcase taking it to the bed and laid it down. He then began to fumble with the latch as he could not keep his eyes off of Tila.

Nicky finally managed to open the suitcase and began laying stuff on the bed. Here are some undergarments and socks, some shirts, a couple of dresses and some shoes. See if you can find something that might fit! Are you alright? Nicky asked yes I feel fine! A little disoriented but I feel fine. I'm going to take a shower and I'll be out in a bit. Nicky said thumbing through a drawer gathering clothes for himself as he closed the door Tila began trying on clothes as she stood in front of the mirror she was finding it very strange to see herself as a human. She began to wonder if Nicky would still find her attractive. She had full voluptuous breasts, her body was slim, her eyes so large they seemed to glow! Her teeth were snow white and her hair was long and curly. As she would try on clothes, she would twirl and bounce around in front of the mirror. She was looking at a pain of under pants not sure what to think and a bra she had never seen before so this she disregarded she found a summer dress it was blue and green and went to just below her knees just as she turned Nicky opened the door to the bathroom stunned by the beauty before him he dropped his towel to the floor! Tila said well how do I look? You, you look so wonderful in a dress he said with a smile stumbling with his words as his heart was beating fast.

The design in the dress and the brightness of the two colors brought out the color of her eyes and the dress clung tight to every curve of her body. He was speechless; he noticed that his mind went back to his fiance as he recalled her wearing that dress often; it was one of her favorites and his heart felt a twang of emptiness.

What do you want to do? Tila said, breaking the thought in Nicky's mind. Well I would say you need some shoes and stuff so we'll go shopping. How's that sound? Can we! She said recalling the store that had clothes displayed in the window so it shall be, Nicky said in a giddy sort of tone, let me finish getting dressed and we'll be on our way! As Nicky was preparing to leave Tila was looking at herself in the mirror. She could hardly believe what she saw! She had never pictured herself as a human and therefore could not or did not know what to expect. Her skin was soft and her hair had the radiance she had always had her legs seem so long yet her height was at about 5'5 tall and maybe 125 in weight her skin was dark and her eyes shone like jewels in the light her lips were full and her voice was quiet yet not shy.

She felt good about herself and hoped that Nicky felt good about her also as Nicky was preparing to leave he couldn't help but to think about how Tila looked as he turned and saw her lying quietly she was even more beautiful than he could have ever imagined she laid there her long curly hair clinging to her dark lean body bronze in color her features were definite and radiant. The little hairs on her skin shone like a layer of haze over her body. Her eyes were sparkling and large, very much aware! Her voice was like a soft melody against his ears. He was feeling excited to be a part of her life. And that she was a part of his, he also knew that he felt a closeness to this woman like he had not felt for some-time and she seemed to feel a part of that towards him! He would take her to dinner after shopping and take it from there. Right now they should get her some clothes to wear. As he approached Tila his heart seemed to beat faster and his breathing became erratic for she was absolutely breathtaking. Are you ready? Yes I am Tila said lets be on our way.

As they hit the streets of town Tila was so excited she could not keep her mind from racing and her eyes from looking for something to do! Everything looked so much different than it did when she was small. The windows of the various merchandise were full of stuff that caught her eyes! She wanted to stop at all of them and explore a few doors down from the clothing store that was an Ice cream store.

Nicky led her inside saying this will be a very sweet treat Nicky ordered them a couple of ice cream cones she saw him licking it and began herself! Mmm she said as she began to eat the cone. It's wonderful what is it, its ice cream made from milk, sugar and ice.

I hoped you would like she said as Nicky reached up and wiped some off the side of her mouth running down her chin. Tila's ice-cream was gone by the time they reached the clothing store and Nicky was finishing his last bite as they walked in. Tila was gone when Nicky turned around. He saw her down an aisle where there were many different colored dresses. The merchant approached Nicky to see if there was anything she could do to help. Smiling, Nicky said my friend Tila would like to try some clothes on to purchase. I would be more than happy to help your friend, the merchants said with a smile! As Nicky walked over to look at the various things stacked neatly in a display case. the merchant approached Tila with curiosity! For Tila was smelling the cloth to the clothes and rubbing it against the side of her face! And on occasion trying to taste a berry or fruit that was painted on a dress is there anything I could help you to try on the merchant asked! Oh yes may I said Tila with anticipation in her voice.

Show me what you are interested in and we'll see if we can find something in your size. As Nicky wandered through the store he could hear Tila giggling and laughing along with making sounds that came with overwhelming excitement and joy. It brought a warm feeling to his heart and a smile to his face. On occasion she would rush up to him and ask him what he thought and there were times when he could do no more than stand there with a grin from ear to ear, Tila would say "I take that as a yes" and off she'd go humming and prancing down the Aisle. Nicky wasn't sure how much time had passed but it was time for the store to close and he was sure the merchant would not keep the store open any longer for them. Both Nicky and Tila thanked the merchant and headed to Nicky's house. The air was crisp and fresh, the moon shone brightly and the stars were sparkling against a midnight blue sky. As they walked home Nicky listened to all Tila had to say about her first shopping adventure and how it was so much fun and found it very hard to choose the items she had. Upon entering the house Nicky showed Tila a couple empty drawers in his dresser for her clothing and he showed her how to hang stuff in the closet on hangers. Also he explained the functions of the bath and shower to Tila she chose to take a bath. Nicky put some of his bath bubbles in the tub.

He lit a couple of candles and dimmed the light in the bathroom for her. He then went to the stereo and turned on some soft music and began to make dinner as Tila approached him and kissed him on the cheek saying thank you for today as she headed toward the bathroom. Nicky watched her as she walked away. He then turned and continued cooking. As Tila entered the bathroom she first noticed the candle the flame were dancing about as the light flickered about the wall she also noticed the candles were filling the bathroom with a flowery fragrance then she noticed the tub was full of bubbles and smiled for Nicky had mentioned one time about this to her and she found it very sweet of him as she begin to undress and step into the tub.. The water was warm and she laid back and relaxed as her body soaked in the relief of the excitement of the day.

She closed her eyes and recalled every minute of her shopping adventure as she bathed. Nicky was busy hustling around the house setting the table, lighting candles and arranging the flowers and setting the plates. Tonight he had fixed fried sea perch and potatoes and asparagus decorating the plates with a slice of orange one strawberry and some parsley he was just setting the last of the food on the table as he heard Tila come out of the bathroom with a long night shirt she had purchased ending just above her knees she had her hair hanging down her shoulder the curls shining from the wetness her face aglow as she spotted the table prepared for dinner it smells so good she said as she sat in her chair, after they ate Nicky made himself a bed on the couch tucked Tila in his bed and kissed her on the forehead good night. There he turned to the couch and sat there watching Tila as sleep grabbed her eyes.

Chapter 21

She was soon completely asleep. What is it that I feel about her? He asked himself if he recalled how he felt when he thought they would never see each other again. My heart was empty and I felt a loss, he recalled. It was a feeling he had experienced at the loss of his fiancé of course that was a feeling he had never had to face and therefore probably related it to the absence of Tila and the realization of what can be. She touched every sense of him and brought back emotions he had wondered if he would ever feel again. She gave him butterflies and made his mind go blank every once in a while just for looking at her. He recalled her giddiness and active attitude and wondered if it would or had changed. There she lay sound asleep and he truly had to tell himself she meant more to him than anything else in the world. He was definitely falling in love with her! He laid his head down and fell fast asleep! Tila was awake as the birds began to sing with the dawning of the day The air was crisp and fresh and she stood before the window, engulfed in the colors than painted the sky with what seemed enhanced beauty as the sun reached above the mountain tops to replace the dark fading hue of evening.

The bees began to race back and forth seeking their need for pollen and what other adventures they sought a morning dove cood it caused to the melody of a brand new day. She quietly dances around the house stopping at the mirror to admire the woman she had become. She noticed Nicky's reflection from upon the couch. He was a very special person she thought and he seemed so much more an attractive man now that she was human. The thought of him and the sight of him as he lay there made her feel things she had never noticed feeling before. There was something inside her she could not define yet she did know that as far as she was concerned he was very much a part of her life, a part she did not ever want to be without. She too recalled the possibility he might not be there in her life.

And how afraid she was when he was attacked by the puma. She could not catch her breath as she recalled that moment. Shaking the image from her mind, she stood in front of the fireplace looking at the picture of Nicky's deceased fiance She wondered if he could feel the same way for her; she sensed his feelings as he spoke of his loss. she recalled the look of pain upon his face and in his voice she knew she would never want to hurt him. She looked upon him and felt warm inside. She ran a finger down the side of his face and smiled. She turned on the phonograph and began arranging the bed she had slept in good morning! Nicky said startling Tila a little bit she turned with a smile. Good morning she said as she admired Nicky sitting up on the couch. Wiping the sleep from his eyes with his hair sticking out in many directions. It brought a low laugh to her throat. Nick thought what a sight to behold first thing in the morning.

I was just preparing for the day Tila said! And ending with a question: what are we going to do today? How would you like to go out for breakfast? Nicky asked heading to the bathroom to wash his face and wet his hair. Are we going out to pick berries? She asked, laughing out loud Nicky said no a restaurant? She inquired yes said Nicky. It is a place where you go and sit down at a table while people ask you what you want. They tell someone who cooks it and then someone brings it to you! That sounds like fun she said I will get dressed would you like the bathroom Nicky asked no I will be fine right here she said as she removed her night shirt blushingly Nicky walked to the drawer and grab some clothes before returning to the restroom After he got dressed he inquired threw the door to make sure she was dressed before he came into the living room.

It's okay! Tila told him. Entering the living room Nicky noticed she had chosen a pair of levis with sandal type shoes and a bright yellow belly button high short sleeved shirt. it seemed to make her glow with happiness. Taking a deep breath, Nicky told her how lovely she looked this morning. The comment and his conclusions of his feelings toward her last night made his cheeks fluster somewhat red and warm. After cleaning the couch and tidying up the house they headed off toward the restaurant. The sun was warm on them as they walked down the street Tila saw people rushing to and fro. She also noticed the children as mothers hollered after them. dogs and cats scurried around the building and ripped at each other in play. She begin laughing out loud as Nicky became aware of the dog she was watching chase his tail going frantically in circles.

And standing totally dazed as it would stop when it lost track of it only to see it again and return to chasing it in circles. Nicky could not help but to laugh with her. She had that kind of laughter! Just as they were about to enter the restaurant Tila saw two children running down the street apparently trying to get away from something chasing them. She made a startled sound that immediately spun Nicky around in deep concern. What is it Tila he asked We need to help those children she warned Nicky there being chased and are screaming to run faster. As Nicky looked he realized what she was seeing and began to laugh very hysterically until he noticed the hurt anger in Tilas eyes then it broke to a snicker as he explained what they were doing. She also began to laugh asking if they could try that Nicky said of course will get a couple of kites right after breakfast! They continued to laugh as they entered the restaurant and took a seat.

The waitress brought them a menu, went over the special of the morning and gave them water! She said she would return shortly to accept their orders. some things she had never heard of such as sausage pancakes omelets corn beef hash etc. so after letting Nicky know that this was an obstacle for her he said if I may I shall order for both of us. Would you like eggs? He asked yes that would be fine she replied! As the waitress approached Nicky began to order we'll have two vegetable omelets with hash browns and wheat toast and one side of bacon please. Anything to drink the waitress asked? Orange juice please he said acknowledging the not from Tila and the waitress hurried off to the kitchen hollering out the order they had gave upon receiving their food Tila expressed how good her meal was.

She made a sour face as she drank her orange juice. Together they sat and enjoyed their meals and each other's company with laughter and joy. After eating, Nicky paid for the meal and Tipped the waitress. As Tila looked on as he did so he told her he would explain can we get what the children had? Tila asked of course Nicky said we shall go to the hardware store across the street. Can I help you the man asked as he walked from behind the counter Where are your kites? Nicky asked over here at the end of this aisle he replied! As Tila and Nicky approached the wall that had a display of ready to fly kites and some rolled up in paper bundles Tila was excited as she noticed the many different colors and how bright they were. Some had an assortment of pictures on them like dragons and snakes, some were just different colored designs. They all looked to be very nice. Nicky chose a dragon and Tila chose one with butterflies and field flowers. They each grabbed a ball of string and paid the gentleman at the counter and off to a field at the end of town they went.

Tila could see the two children she had seen their kites very far up in the sky as they approached the field. "Look" they heard the little girl say as they approached they have kites also" Nicky began to lay his kite open out on the ground and encouraged Tila to do the same. Tila copied what she saw Nicky doing as he tied the ends of the pieces of sticks provided to the corners of the kites paper he continued by tying the stickers where they intersect on the back side of the paper part of the kites he then helped Tila when it came to tying the string to create a bow in the cross piece of wood and the string with slack upon the face side of the kite which the ball of string was attached.

Nicky then pulled out the piece of ribbon to tie to the bottom of the kite for balance. after helping Tila with a few last details he asked her if she was ready yes I'm ready" she replied Nicky laid her kite on an open flat as he backed up 10-15 yards letting sting out from the spool he began to explain to Tila what was necessary to get the kite in the air, as he explained it she broke out in hysterical laughter. I was just recalling how I felt as the children were running down the road with their kites behind them. Nicky chuckled and reminded her as it began to rise in the air to let out string. The breeze was mild but constant. Tila began running, giggling as she went the kite rose swiftly Tila turned around and let the string out until the kites were well above their heads except for the swaying back and forth. The kites were steady Nicky too had his kite in flight and had worked his way to Tila.

Tila gasped as Nicky's kite flew close to hers he showed her how if she pulled the string one way or another the kite would fly in different directions and spin circles the soon were both dodging each other laughing and making challenges a gust of wind caught the kites and Tilas kite headed straight for the ground oh! No! She called out, gave it a little slack and then pull on the string quickly. As she did her kite turned upward and began to climb. I did it, she said with excitement. They flew kites the rest of the afternoon till they were exhausted. Bringing the kites down. rolling up the string proved to be a little tough for Tila. Then Nicky showed her how to get the kite on the ground first. Thank you she said as she finished with the string and walked up to Nicky with the kite behind her it made me miss flying. She told Nicky are you okay he asked as she was obviously missing her home at that moment. It occurred to Nicky it might be good to take a walk in the forest after dinner. The wind blew warm in their faces as they walked back to the house. Talking about the kite flying experience.

Chapter 22

Tila was so excited it took her awhile to relax from the thrill of flying the kites. Yet she seemed to feel the exhaustion of the fun as she relaxed stretching across the couch as Nicky got them both a glass of ice water. As he sat on the floor next to her. "Well"! Tila I was thinking we should go out for dinner tonight and we could take a walk through the forest afterwards, if you would like. The forest! She said aloud, you mean the forest? Yes I certainly do the very same oh could we Nicky? I would enjoy that! I was hoping you would feel that way! "Let me wash up and change my clothes" Nicky said and "I'll be ready" I'll wash up in here Tila replied as she hurried to the bed to get a change of clothes. A few minutes later they walked out the door and were on their way as Nicky helped Tila with her jacket. The breeze had picked up some so they had arrived at the wharf for dinner fairly fast. As they entered Tila noticed the big nets on the wall with large glass balls and fishing poles and stuffed fish entwined in the netting.

You could smell the salt air mixed with the seafood being cooked on an open grill and every once in a while the sweet smell of wine. Being manually crushed in the back room of the restaurant. As they sat they could look out the window and see the boats that were stationary and those that were either on their way out to sea or just coming back from sea. One could see the waves crashing onto the shore and caressing the sand as it returned to the vastness of the ocean. The seagulls followed the boats back and forth and flew off the docks as people walked to shore. The waitress brought them some small loafs of bread with honey butter. Wrapped in a basket covered by a checkered cloth to keep it warm. This was complemented by a bowl of clam chowder. Nicky could see Tilas eyes sparkle as the candle light reflected in them. Nicky's heart- felt so happy and the smile was unstoppable. You could see the joy in her face and it was something that all the riches in the world could not even come close to comparing to. The world was without substance as he looked at her and he was happy! After their meal a seafood platter they had a few drinks and figured it time to head on out to the forest.

Tila giggled as she felt light head from the wine they had with dinner. Nicky covered Tilas shoulders as they headed down the road. The conversation at first was over dinner, how sweet the butter was, how wonderful the crab and lobster was and how awkward and messy it seemed to be to eat, Nicky assured her that was how it was supposed to be. Tila began to flood Nicky with one question after another mostly about the boats she saw coming in and out of the bay. The boxes she saw being unloaded and the many other things she saw. Just as they entered the forest they were startled by a bird that flew from the branch of a large pine. Looking up Nicky recognized the bird to be Brier, the owl. "Brier" he called out as the owl circled heading back in their direction "it's me and Tila"! Nicky said out loud "yes it's true"! Tila called out Nicky, Tila Brier said with reservation, how could it be? It is magic just as I was able to be small so is Tila able to be human. You are beautiful Brier said to Tila. I would have never known or believed if I had not seen it with my own two "able I might add" eyes he exclaimed. I was wondering why I haven't seen you "I figured you had gone to see your mother" Brier said. I must tell the others because I'm sure they would be very excited to see you as you are. Why you're so, well you're so big! He said shyly. Yes! That would be great. Nicky said in fact we were just heading to the pond to sit on the big rock and wait for the moon.

Tell them we shall be there waiting to see them. Yes, I shall be on my way! I shall return as soon as I am able. Thank you Nicky and Tila said almost simultaneously and Tila giggled as she hurried down the path she had spent her life flying down. Calling back a Nicky I bet I beat you there! Surprised by the head start Nicky sprinted down the path hollering I'll catch you as he sped to catch up. As he approached the rock Tila was teasing him with taunts of "what took you so long" and did you stop to smell the flowers, Nicky laughed as he reach to catch hold of Tila as she dodged his grasp and darted to one side, I'm going to catch you Nicky said chasing her thru the bushes and around the rock and pond. As he lost sight of Tila he paused to look and she grabbed him by his legs and tackled him to the ground as he tried to tickle her to get away.

They laid in the grass by the pond laughing at one another hello! They heard as they looked across the short distance of the pond. Here Nicky said! As he looked to see there on the rock was Cheal, Huey, and Justin the raccoon. All turning to look Nicky's way. Tila began to stand as she saw all their eyes become larger in a giggle tone she spoke to them hey guys! It's me jTila you don't have to look so shocked! You look so different Cheal said yea what Cheal said Huey replied. You look different, you're so big, where are your wings Justin asked, can I have them?. No silly Tila said you cannot have my wings! As she walked towards them. I've missed you all so much it seems forever since I've seen you yet I realize it has not! As she approached the rock and sat down they backed up a little and began sniffing at her.

They were soon upon her lap as she caressed and petted them almost at the same time, they were so excited to see her. Justin ran down the side of the rock and returned quickly with a very shiny rock he had found earlier during the day. It was freshly washed thank you Tila said as she held it up to look at it. Well I'll be! If I hadn't seen it with my own eyes I would have never believed it! Although I'm not sure I do even as I approach! I will know if this is some kind of trick! I know Tila very well and if this is a test I will pass it and I will conclude the truth Jason! Jason! Tila said it, is me! I am human! Human, why would you want to go and do something like that! No offense Nicky. None taken, Nicky said with a smile. It's temporary, Nicky said! Good Jason said as he began to eye Tila with examining interest you make a very viewable human if in fact it is you! I assure you it is me Jason! Tioga made it possible so I could see Nicky's world as he saw my world and was able to fly. You are very attractive I suppose! For a human Jason said. Will you come back home he asked? Why yes! I'm having a very good time though and there is so much I want to do. She said they sat and listened as she told of things she saw and of flying kites and shopping! As they listened intently Brier flew in and landed on a branch above Tila and Nicky's head. I could not find anybody else he said even Tioga was off somewhere.

Tila backed up some and recalled a few things to update Brier and continued on as to how she was looking forward to being on a boat and a train she explained the horse and buggies. The many shops and all they had within them Justin listened with open ears as his mind wandered visualizing all the shiny possibilities such treasures he thought. Cheal and Huey were picking at each other taunting one another it was so nice to be around her friends as she picked up Huey and petted Cheal between his ears, Justin had his head on her lap as he listened and dreamed of all she had spoke of what a collection he thought it was getting dark as Nicky and Tila prepared to leave everyone walked them to the edge of the forest and waved goodbye as the moon begin to rise above the mountain and the sun begin to set. Nicky reached out and held Tila's hand as the headed back to the house. Not a word was hardly spoken until they reached the door. Thank you Nicky Tila said, Thank you very very much she repeated as she reached up and kissed him very gently on his cheek.. And walked into the house Nicky just stood there not wanting to lose the moment. I am tired Tila said as she laid down on the bed Nicky went into the bathroom and when he came out Tila was sound asleep! He smiled and covered her up with a blanket and laid himself on the couch. Goodnight he said aloud an fluffed his pillow and dosed off

Chapter 23

Nicky began to toss and turn as he slept the water was rough and the waves began to swell as the wind blew and the rain fell faster he could feel it sting on his face like hundreds of tiny needles it was cold and his hand were numb he could hardy hold on to the line tied to the bow of the ship. He hollered for her but there was no answer. The boat began to sway from side to side and the mast and crow's nest would lay against the crashing waves as they washed over the ship pulling what they could to an angry sea! As he yelled out he saw her rise out to the deck from below frantically searching as their eyes met the boat struck hard against something jarring them both to the deck and forward as the wave covered the boat again he grabbed her hand and the boat went completely over. She was slipping from his frozen grasp; he was losing her as the ocean pulled her; he screamed her name and he awoke to a startle. Nicky are you alright? He opened his eyes and he could feel the sweet beaded on his forehead as he saw Tila, eyes wide with fear and concern.

Oh Tila he said as he looked around to make sure all was real his heart was still pounding he stood pulling Tila close and squeezing her tight OH Tila! He said again are you alright she repeated! Yes, yes, I am fine now. I was having a bad dream! But I'm alright now. What time is it? As she looked at the clock it was 3am as Tila sat on the couch she pulled Nicky's head to her shoulder and ran her fingers through his hair and said it will be alright. Together they laid back against the arm of the couch and fell asleep again. Tila awoke to the sound of the teapot whistling; she could smell the mint tea Nicky was steeping in the cups and could smell the bacon toast. She smelled and yawned, `` aren't we looking pert this morning! She taunted him and turned to smirk at her and said would you like your tea as you shower yes thank you! Was her reply as she grabbed a cup with sleepy morning eyes and off to the bathroom.

Smiling, he turned back to the toast that was finished waiting to be buttered. He laid the honey butter he had bought from the restaurant on the table. He knew it would be a welcome surprise as would be him suggesting a trip to the city to meet his mother. Which meant traveling on the train. Tila looking as beautiful as ever sat at the table as they talked about how nice it was to see all her friends at the pond she wish she could have seen Tioga and Jazmin but she would see them soon but it didn't stop her from missing them as she stared into her second cup of tea. Nicky broke the silence as he asked her if she would like to go on a train ride as he knew she would without hesitation excited and eager. Oh! I would love to meet your mother, she added asking when they would go! Soon he said we must pack and get tickets I think we can leave as soon as tomorrow evening

What should I take? What should I wear? Is there anything I should do? Think she'll like me? I'm sure she will, Nicky said with a smile! Everything will be alright. We'll have plenty to do, Nicky said as he poured some more water for tea and took a bite of his bacon.

The rest of the day was very much eventful they had clothes to pack a couple of trips to the store and they were able to get travel kits of toothpaste toothbrushes, deodorant, personal thing for Tila and a few more clothing items Tila was overjoyed with the idea. And it made him feel so good. So many things that we take for granted she found as treasures and would marvel at with such child-like enthusiasm. She was full of questions. Especially about the city there was so much she could hardly imagine then he told her of the opera and theaters.

She became speechless with that special glitter in her eye that would compare to a child's Christmas morning. Together they went to the train station. Nicky walked her around and showed her the transfer station where the trains would add cars and line up on the right tracks for their destinations. She saw the steam that came from engines as the whistle blew and the smoke as the train would move back and forth. She saw the conductors as they waved their lights. Some had red ones and some had green ones and some had lamps that were both red and green. Nicky explained the red was for stop and green was for go. He showed her how the track was switched by pulling a large lever so as to change the course of the train as they entered the booth. Nicky asked for two tickets, paid for them and went home. Nicky told Tila about all the things she would see, And the tunnels that went through the mountains and bridges that went over deep canyons and over large rivers. She listened with interest and questions as they entered the house. Their train would be leaving tomorrow night at dusk so they had time to go by and see Tioga in the morning before they left. Tila just wouldn't want to go without seeing him if she could help it and Nicky agreed so it was set they would leave right after breakfast but tonight they would relax. Nicky would go out and get some Chinese food and bring it home so they wouldn't have to cook! He also got a couple pair of chopsticks he could try to teach Tila to use them that brought a chuckle to him by the time he had returned Tila had finished with her bath and was dressed in a dark purple silk nightgown that was somewhat short but she had shorts that was a part of it she was as usual most beautiful.

I brought dinner, he said as he put plates on the table and began serving them up! When he was finished he laid the chop sticks next to the plates he had bought shrimp, rice, and chow mein, with pot sticker's it is a noodle with meat in them as they sat to eat. Nicky lit the candles. This is wonderful Tila said as she picked up the sticks next to her plate chopsticks he said as he put them between his fingers and closed them on a piece of shrimp. She put them in her hands as he showed her how to hold them when she was able to get them to open and close. She attempted to grab some shrimp just as she got it off her plate the sticks twisted and the shrimp went flying past Nicky. She covered her mouth as she laughed and he reached around and picked it up setting it on the table she continued to try and soon was able to get some in her mouth.

All the time she giggled with enjoyment although she wasn't getting full very fast. She was having fun. She eventually abandoned the chopsticks and ate her food with a fork. It was very good and soon they were both full and Nicky had poured them some champagne he bought at the store. It tickled as it went down and soon had them both relaxed. They sat on the bed together and talked of all the fun they've had and how there were times when she missed home but was having so much fun. Tomorrow she would see Tioga and then they would be on their way to the city. As they became tired they said their goodnights and settled down to sleep. They both were deep in thought as they became more tired. Nicky tried to cover everything that was needed in his head so they would not forget anything and Tila was thinking of seeing Tioga tomorrow and wondered how he would react to the way she looked now. She recalled how her friends had reacted.

They both laid there watching the light from the fireplace flicker off the walls until their eyes closed for the evening. The next morning found them heading into the forest as the sun began to rise, the birds were singing their songs and the creatures of the night were scurrying to make it to their homes before the day became too warm and to get their rest before the evening returned as they came to the waterfall Tila said she hadn't noticed the place quit this ways as a fairy. It didn't seem as far up to where Tioga lived she called out his name and was answered in a grumbled voice over here. As they turned they saw Tioga coming up the trail he had been picking fruit, flowers, and herbs. Well my! My! My! He said as he noticed Nicky and approached Tila, aren't we a beautiful human he said with a smile I would have never noticed it was you had I not seen Nicky! How are you?

Tila asked fine, thank you how is everything going? She said she too was doing fine and was having so much fun. She knelt to hold Tioga in her hand and tell him she missed him he told her the others had said they saw her. They visited me and I was informed you were going to the city to meet Nicky's mother. Tioga reminded her of everything he told her the last time they were at his house getting the potion. Especially how important it was that they both remember this can only be done three times, but the third time is permanent. It was time for them to be heading back and Tila made it clear she would remember all she was told. Reassuring Tioga she set him gently on the ground as they said their goodbyes. They both kept their eyes open for Jazmin, yet neither one of them had seen so much as a sight she might be near.

Of course she was a very cautious puma and the smell of humans carried a long way. How was she to recognize Tila like this? The sun was warm and then they left the shadows of the forest. The reservation of leaving her friends behind was soon replaced with the excitement and eagerness to be on their way. "We must get our luggage to the station". Said Nicky then we can grab a bite to eat before leaving. "I am kind of hungry," she said. Seems to me humans sure do eat a lot. "Yes we do," Nicky said humorously. We should make some sandwiches and put some snacks together for the train ride. "We could have like a little picnic on the train" said Tila with a smile while they were in the house Nicky gathered up the gear for the trip that was to be put in the cargo box of the train and Tila put together a basket of food, in case they got hungry. Together they went to the train station and got something to eat before leaving.

Chapter 24

Upon entering the train Nicky showed Tila the dining car then took her back to the caboose to see the end of the train. She was able to take a look at the engine, before they boarded. She saw the man shoveling black rock which Nicky explained was coal. She also saw the engineer "it's so large" she said Tila was also impressed by the many people in the passenger car. She had no idea so many traveled this way. they took their seats Nicky let Tila, sit by the window so she could look at the scenery. She heard the conductor "all aboard" he said as the whistle blew with a startling loudness the cars began to jerk forward as one pulled on the other. Soon the train was in a steady motion forward as one pulled on the other. Soon the train was in a steady forward motion and they were on their way. Nicky had made this trip a few times but he never really recalled the last time he took the time to admire the sites along the way. If you watch closely, Nicky advises Tila you might see some deer and bear, maybe some buffalo along the way. "How wonderful," she replied. Things began to go by faster as she caught sight of the forest. It was so large and seemed to go on forever. The trees were so tall, and thick she could not see the pond or the waterfall. Tila watched with enthusiasm and the train rolled along. Nicky began to tell her about where he grew up as a child and all the while she listened with interest. He told of his school days and the many summers he spent swimming and fishing after explaining in detail some of his outdoor adventures Tila was interested in sitting by the lake with a fire while fishing. Nicky added that to his mental list of things he wanted to do with her.

Tila was surprised as they traveled there were times when she would not see a single tree. All she could see was strange looking stumps and shrugs. Nicky explained to her that it was desert land and their stumps were cactus. She had never seen or even imagined a place without trees. One time they were crossing over a large river and Nicky had pointed out a mamma bear and her two cubs on the bank of the river. They had seen many deer and elk. At one time there was a Golden Eagle that flew alongside the train for some distance. Look! Tila said with surprise there is a large hole in the mountain and we're headed right for it! That is one of the tunnels I was telling you about as they entered the tunnel the lights on the wall of the passenger car were visible.

There was just enough light to be able to see clearly outside the window. It was pitch black, It seem to go on forever as Tila watched out the window. Soon she was able to see light against the wall as they headed toward the opening that exited the tunnel. Soon they were back in the sunlight rounding the mountain they had just gone through. Then they were going through the forest as the conductor announced they would be stopping for a short moment to pick up mail and equipment to be delivered to the city. As they stopped people unloaded and some people loaded, there were animals like cows and sheep being unloaded. Some of the creates were the same as the ones Tila had noticed being unloaded at the docks back home. I see things can be transported for. Between boats and trains. "Yes they can" said Nicky airplanes play a big part in stuffed being shipped great distances also.

The train ride was not a real long one but there was plenty to see. The closer they got the more nervous Nicky was and the more anxious Tila felt. As it began to get darker the stars began to show and Tila would look into the sky and think of what might come tomorrow. Would Nicky's mom like her, would they approve of her being with him, she sure hopes so. Her ears become tuned to the rhythm of the train rolling down the track as her mind seems to shut down from exhaustion; her head tilted toward Nicky's shoulder as he moved closer to her allowing her to rest more comfortably. As Nicky rested his eyes he could smell the fragrance of Tilas hair and felt at ease.

They were both awakened by the sound of the train's whistle as the conductor moved from car to car announcing the next arrival "Be sure to gather all your belongings if this is your destination. Also he announced the departure to other destinations further down the line. The cars clanged together with a jerk of the train as it came to a stop. As the doors opened people began to embark upon the platform awaiting the removal of their luggage. Nicky stepped off of the train. Turning to help Tila down she stood there looking with great excitement as she saw the many people scurrying around, the large brightly colored buildings It reminds me of a beehive in spring time" she said as she took Nicky's hand and stepped down. It is so large and there are so many people! As she looked around she saw people of many different cultures of all shapes and sizes. All dressed differently from rather warm looking clothes to long black coats with white shirts and ties. Women in dresses made with material more colorful than a rainbow. And hats that looked as if someone had planted an herb and flower garden on them.

Tila almost felt dizzy as she caught herself going in circles trying to take it all in. Nicky retrieved their luggage and stood next to Tila. Are you ready to go? "Oh yes"! She replied I want to see more. Together they began to walk down the wooden dock to the road. Horseless carriages and buggies were cautiously making their way down roads as people crossed them making their way to destinations nearby. The sidewalks were also busy with children and people who were casually frequenting the establishments at hand. There were many window which displayed many items from personal, home, and recreation, work and other novelties which people might find or need for.

Nicky could only smile as he watched Tila examine each window one by one with equal enthusiasm and desire. He was pretty sure if she had her way her arms would be full with bags of things she desired. There were hustlers marketing various items that were newly available people with stands, selling fruits, fish, cheese, meats, and handmade trinkets. "This is so wonderful" Tila said as she held Nicky's hand raising her shoulder in a joyful childish way. So much we take for granted Nicky thought as he tried to imagine seeing so much at once one had never even known existed. So many things he had never noticed and probably would not have had it not been for Tila and her wonderful enthusiasm. How much of life actually just passed us by that we never see because we are so narrowly focused or how much is not appreciated because we are busy looking for something better.

Instead of enjoying and being happy and content in what we already have? Nicky was so glad she was a part of his life and he knew at that moment that he did not want to be without her. As they continue to walk down the sidewalk Tila continues to be fascinated by the sounds and smells that seem to come from everywhere. They stopped as they came across some nuns on the side of the walkway singing. The harmony was low yet attractive to the ear. AS they finished Nicky and Tila began the last short distance to Nicky's mothers house.

Chapter 25

As they turned off the busy streets they were walking down a more quiet and peaceful road the traffic was less by far. Children playing here and there laughing and chasing each other. The sides of the roads were lined with large beautifully full trees, and flowers seemed to be everywhere, some lined pathways that led to houses. Others were in boxes under windows and along steps and porches. The spring air was sweet with their fragrance as the morning began anew. A lonely buggy pulled by horses approached slowly as it stopped at various houses leaving white bottles filled with milk for those who purchased them. This he explained to Tila. "We're almost there,'" he told her. He had noticed as he became more excited to see his mother, Tila became quieter and somewhat passive. He could sense her nervousness.

Nicky looked her way and smiled. She returned it as she put her arms to his waist. "This is beautiful," she said in a low, sincere tone. They turned and began walking up the walkway to a white house with a dark roof and blue trim. There was a mailbox hanging next to the screen door. Two white pillars held the awning above the steps to the house and then there was a pine tree that grew in the front yard. The door came open as they neared the steps to the house. The woman who opened the door was smiling. Her face was wrinkled with a smooth outline that expressed joy and love. Her silver hair was rolled in a bun on the backside of her head. She approached Tila with an extended hand that was soft and warm yet strong to the touch.

"Hi mom" Nicky said as he set the bags down and hugged her "this must be Tila" she said excited to see her. I have heard alot about you my dear. Welcome, welcome please come in. I had not expected you to come in so early and I shall fix you both some breakfast. Nicky grabbed the bags and the bottle of milk off the porch as he followed his mother who had her arm over Tilas shoulder leading her into the house. The house was not very large by no means as one entered the door you were in the living room and dining room which led to a kitchen with a food storage room that was small as one walked through the living room, the hallway led to a small and large bedroom and bathroom. The backyard was closed in by a fence with a clothes line that ran near the length of the back yard. It was cozy and well kept. There was plenty of light that showed in the windows that were located in every room. The sofa was covered by a quilt made of many pieces of material in many different colors and designs. The lamp on the end table was covered with a shade that gave the appearance of a mountain scene with running water. While the light en-hance every chair in the room, and a large round rug that covered the floor. Please have a seat. Nicky's mother said to them both you must be hungry" as she rushed into the kitchen.

I shall get something started. How was your Trip? "Fine! thanks" Nicky replied. Nicky wanted to tell his mother it was Tila's first train ride, He just did not know how to explain why if the question arises. "This is Tila's first time in the city" He managed to say. So what do you think she asked Tila. By the way "you may call me mom she said that's what I'm used to answering to" she said as she shuffled pans on the stove. "It's very large and full of people" she said looking at Nicky. He just smiled and said it's okay! I can see how that could be It didn't take long for a hot breakfast to be setting on the table. Nicky sat next to Tila and mom sat in her usual spot at the end where she has always sat. That allowed her to face the family equally. As she sat with a content smile the two of them dished up bacon, eggs, and potatoes toast was buttered with home churned butter and various jams were placed on a tray for use. "This is very good," Tila replied! "How long will you stay"? Mom asked Nicky. I figured I would stay at least a couple of days. "It will be so nice"! Mom said. Especially since it seems I already know you Tila! Nicky has told me so much and talks about you all the time.

There is a carnival in town mom gestured toward a flier she received at her door. It starts tomorrow Nicky, maybe we could all go down and show Tila some of the big city life. Sounds like fun to me mom! Tila said the same and smiled shyly as she ate. After breakfast they put their luggage in Nicky's old bedroom and made sure all was well for Tila to sleep there. Her clothes were put in drawers and Nicky said he would sleep on the floor. The sun was out and it was going to be a lovely day. Mom had some errands to run and some shopping to do and suggested meeting the kids in town for lunch. Nicky had suggested going to the park and zoo for a while this morning, and Tila was eagerly waiting to be on the way. So they agreed to meet at noon to have lunch.

As mom left for town Tila approached Nicky. "Do you think she likes me"? She asked. Of course she does, everything is okay! She is very happy to have you here. This is so wonderful she told Nicky as she embraced him in her arms. Kissing his face. I am so glad to be here with you. I am glad! You! Are with me he replied, squeezing her back with great emotion and pride. Shall we explore the city he said as he grabbed her hand and walked out the door. It was another beautiful day as they walked down the walk way, leaves from the trees glided gently to the ground, giving way the gentle blowing breeze. As always the children were everywhere playing, laughing, tossing balls and chasing each other. Just as they approached the main street to the city Tila was stopped in awe as she tried to absorb the fascination of the seemingly chaos before her.

She had never seen so many people in one area before. It was as the world gathered together in one spot. There was no comparison to what she had seen early that morning. Business was booming and the streets were busy with buggies drawn by beautiful horses and not even back home while flying above the forest had she seen so much activity as she witnessed. She could see games set up in booths, throwing axes, cutting logs, horse racing, foot races, buggy races, men that seem to be fighting in an enclosed area for all to see. Men, women and children cheering out loud for their pick of each individual contest. The smell of food was everywhere as vendors hustled their goods, jams, jelly', pies, and donuts were all for tasting and judging. Every now and then the distinct smell of alcohol as bars were set up as longboards over barrels of beer, wine and some that made Tilas' eyes water at the smell. So many different styles of food that she seemed full just from tasting not all was tolerable there were some she secretly would discard hoping no one had seen. Which made Nicky blush as he held back his laughter. Tila was allowed to enter a large tub where women were stomping grapes for wine. She could not keep from giggling as the grapes were squished between her toes. It reminded her of walking along the banks of the river and impoundments at home. As she sat drying her feet, Nicky was making fun of her grape stained legs and feet. I am having so much fun she said what shall we do next.

They were having a potato sack race that Nicky had enlisted Tila and himself in, as Nicky explained it to her she could not wait to get started. Nicky suggested Tying their ankles together and practicing walking around that seemed to go well but awkward, it was their first attempt at running that proved to be the labor of the event. As they would begin to run Tila would begin laughing so hard her eyes would water and she could not concentrate as they would hit the ground she would try to apologize but it made no difference to Nicky, the joy was watching Tila. It didn't take them long to begin moving as one. When it came time for the race they gave it their very best and were more than happy with the small trophies they received for third place. Nicky told Tila how good she had done as he wiped the mud off her face and the grass out of her hair they had both received as they fell over the finish line both laughing hysterically as they recovered the realized that with all the excitement the morning seem to go so swiftly that it was well past time to meet with Nicky's mother for lunch.

They decided to go to the house and relax some before the night fell and be ready to watch the fireworks. Tilas head was filled with the many things she saw and heard. She seems to gaze into the distance trying to absorb it all. Nicky could see the questions pile upon Tilas mind and knew eventually he'd be explaining the day's activities in detail. It could only bring a smile to his face. As he entered the house Nicky's mother had food on the table Tila found her way to the couch as Nicky went in to talk with his mother. She greeted him with a hug as he explained the events of the day and the comical reactions of Tilas. His mother could only laugh. She made some tea as Nicky walked into the living room to give Tila some tea. She was fast asleep. Tila only smiled as Nicky laid a pillow under her head and covered her with a quilt. She is so beautiful he thought to himself and kissed her on the forehead.

Nicky and his mother spent the rest of the afternoon catching up on events since they were last together and they both end the conversation with laughter for the event of the potatoes sack race and of course the winning of the third place trophy which Nicky gave to his mother to save as they sat there to themselves Nicky begin to wonder if he should try to explain Tila to his mother not knowing where to begin he excused himself to nap before the evenings excitement. Nicky's mother went into the kitchen to make them a basket to take with them and folded a blanket for them and set it by the door before she retired to her rocking chair on the porch where she would spend many nights during the warm seasons.

Chapter 26

Nicky awoke to the sound of laughter as he lay there smelling the fresh air and a smile came to his face. Then with a start he became concerned to the fact that the laughter he was hearing was Tila's and his mother. What if she had mentioned anything that would cause his mother to worry about where Tila might be from. Nicky jumps out of bed as he rushes to the doorway pausing to regain his composure before walking onto the porch. As he walked out Tila turned to him saying "your mother was just telling me about you as a child and she was showing me pictures, blushing she said I even saw you when you had lost your draws while running across the yard Mother! Nicky jokingly said that it isn't anything sacred anymore. As they all giggled, about ready to go watch the fireworks, Nicky asked Tila, yes I'm very excited your mother told me how wonderful it was going to be Nicky! Mother said. I had packed a basket for you two and folded a blanket for you all.

I've put it by the door when you're ready to go! Thank you mother they both said at the same time. I'll grab a couple of jackets just in case Nicky suggested as he walked back into the house. Upon securing the coats Nicky set them along with the basket and blanket outside on the porch. Mother, are you going with us? He asked. No, you kids run along. I can see them just fine from here. I will probably be turning in early anyway okay! He said as Tila grabbed the blanket and a jacket. Nicky kissed his mother with a smile as she said have fun! Nicky grabbed the basket and off they went. The fireworks were being lit off at the baseball field which was just down the road by the golf course. Nicky led Tila over a small bridge that crossed a small creek onto the green lawn of the golf course. He laid out their blanket in a place that was about two hundred yards from the baseball field. As Tila looked around she began to question Nicky about the short green grass with the sand bars.

As he began to explain he could see it wasn't going to be easy. So he suggested that he bring her out here tomorrow and let her see for herself. She was content with that as they began to set things out to prepare for the fireworks show. As they went through the basket they had found fried chicken, potato salad, and a selection of sliced fruits and vegetables along with a cooler of sun tea. The smell of the chicken called to Tila's stomach as she began to realize how hungry she was. The food was beginning to hit the spot as the sun had set and darkness laid its vail about the land, Tila was opening the sliced fruit just as the night exploded with a brilliant flash of light that caught her immediate attention yet as startling as the light was the deafening bang that followed was all it took to put the small container of fruit soaring into the air as Tila in a sheer instant was wrapped around Nicky.

Her eyes were as large as silver dollars and yet as much as she was shaking Nicky could still hear her heartbeat. It was his growing interest and feeling for her that wished he would have thought to warn her or something for she had seen the colorful flashes of light and the loud sounds before, but not as close as she now was. Nicky began to tell her she would be alright and explain as she was sitting upright somewhat embarrassed by her reaction. She was into the moment and it was not expected she explained as she saw the next set of fireworks flash high into the sky. Soon they were side by side looking high above themselves as like in a dream the sky was painted over and over again in various colors and shapes the sound of Tilas interest and excitement was providing for the best of times in Nicky recollection. Tila was beautiful in the flashing night as her face glowed and her eyes sparkled. She couldn't say "Did you see that" enough as they would recall each display right after the grand finale.

Where everything seems to go off at once, a show that seems to have no end. The night was warm yet Nicky dropped a coat over Tilas shoulders as the packed and headed back to the house. They both prepared to call it a night as Tila wrapped her arms around Nicky and Kissed him good-night. Goodnight Nicky said see you in the morning as he rubbed the side of his face we her lips seem to leave a tingling impression Tila was soon asleep as she saw over and over the many beautiful loud and overwhelming display of fireworks Nicky lay in bed thinking of how wonderful the day was, Tila was becoming more and more a natural part of his life. The questions seemed endless. How would he explain it to his mother? What was going to happen with them? What was it like for Tila? Did she miss home? She obviously was so overwhelmed by the things she was experiencing that she had no time for much thought at all. They would have to be leaving soon, she would be going back to the forest that thought left an empty feeling in Nickys stomach as it became quite clear how much Tila was a part of his life he would have to be going back to work. He began to think of all the friends back home not around town but around the forest.

He begins to think of how much he shared with Tila. This was a city full of cars, motorcycles, the many many things that were not as accepted by those trying to avoid the claustrophobic lifestyle but to live the simple life where danger didn't lurk around every corner. And people were merely concerned with making a dollar that the valve of life was no longer a matter of importance. Where war was more a marketing strategy than a means of survival. How lucky he thought to be so innocent of such ignorance and dysfunction, the forest was from what he experienced the way life should be as one would read in a fairytale or fantasy fiction book. Yet he knew first-hand the peace and tranquility that the forest held. Yet it also was not without its danger as he recalled his encounter with the wild cat. Or the spider's web somehow the thought of natural dangers seems to have less disgust than those imposed upon by man Nicky soon tired and sleep prevailed.

Tila rolled over as a warm summer night breeze rolled through the window, slightly ruffling her hair. She seemed to be smiling as her mind was reflecting on the events of yesterday. Nicky's image was so real she felt she could reach out and touch him. She had felt so safe in his arms as the explosion of the first firework was set off. She had seen his concern for her feelings as he comforted her. As the night lingered on she felt the gentleness as Nicky's arm held the coat over her as she lay with her head against his chest. He would let her know to watch as he could pre determine the firework about to go off by the popping sound as it left the canister. She was able to follow along once she knew what to listen for. She could recall the softness of the short cut grass as she rubbed the bottom of her feet upon it and walking hand in hand on the way home seemed so natural. She was glad to be here yet she caught herself wondering how things were going at home. She hoped all was well and hoped that Tioga and the rest of her friends were well. It seemed like a very long time since she had thought about them yet it had only been a few days.

She would look forward to going home and sharing her adventure with everyone else, especially the potato sack race. Nicky awoke to the smell of frying bacon as birds chirped outside his window. He had slept well and hoped Tila had also. He heard footsteps outside the door as Tila called his name, breakfast is ready she said. I'll be right there he replied getting dressed he headed to the dining room. The smell of the food definitely aroused his hunger as they ate breakfast. They shared the evening events with his mother. She said she went to bed early but enjoyed what she saw of the fireworks. Nicky explained to mom that he was going to take Tila golfing this morning because the course had aroused her curiosity. Mother said there were still a set of golf clubs in the closet; she also mentioned that they should be just the right size for Tila. Well probably go to the driving range first and see if she might want to try a whole round of gulf. Tila expressed her willingness to try as she finished up the morning meal. Tila said she would be ready as soon as she showered. She enjoyed her showers. The water was so warm and the smell of the soap was like a bed of flowers. Sometimes she felt she could spend all day there.

Nicky had finished his shower and was dressing as Tila knocked on the door. "Come in" he said as he opened the door. "You about ready?" She asked! "Hold your draws on" he said as she looked at the pants she was wearing and shot Nicky an odd glance. It's a figure of speech he told her. Yet she still looked puzzled. I was thinking of home last night. Do you think everything is alright? I had thought of myself he said and assured her all was most likely very much okay. He also brought it to her attention that they would be leaving to go back home tomorrow morning! Thank you she said for what for being you she replied as she hugged him and left the room. He enjoyed it when Tila would show she shared some of the same feelings that he had for her. Nicky had been explaining the fundamentals of golf to Tila as they made their way to the golf course.

So by the time they arrived she had a general idea of what was required. Nicky went inside and paid for a couple of buckets of golf balls. Having explained the different uses of the many clubs pulled a three wood for Tila and a one wood for himself. He showed Tila the movements of the swing. Tila brought the club back behind her and swung the club over the tee where the ball should be as the club came forward it continued on down the range. Tila with the look of shock and embarrassment called to Nicky, but as he looked and saw no club in her hand a broad smile swept over his face as he began to laughing so hard he was holding his stomach, Nicky Tila said out loud as he turned she had thrown a golf ball at him, that as he lifted had hit him solidly on the forehead. Grabbing his head he went to his knees and Tila went from upset to scared and sorry she had thrown the ball at him but it had been a sudden reaction to his laughter at her embarrassment. As she reached Nicky he was still snickering as he rubbed his head. Are you okay? She asked. Yes he said as he explained the look on her face was priceless and began to laugh again, Tila slapped him on the shoulder and went to retrieve her golf club. When she came back she saw a round red mark on his head and apologized again, It's okay he said.

Tila smiled back at him as he said let's see if we can get you hitting the ball. It took a few tries and it wasn't long before she was hitting the ball like she had been at it for sometime. She had a little trouble when she made the change to irons but soon caught on. They spent the next 3 hours working their way around the course. The water and sand traps proved to be a problem for both of them but they enjoyed themselves immensely. They enjoyed a snack at the deli nearby. We have a few things to do before we head back home. So we'll get started for the house and prepare for our train trip home.

Chapter 27

The rest of the afternoon was spent getting things gathered up and put in suitcases. Mom stayed busy in the kitchen making sure they had plenty to eat and some fresh sun tea. While they traveled on the train. After all was done they sat around and ate popcorn while they talked and watched television. Tila found television somewhat baffling; she could not see how all those people could fit inside such a small box. She had to fight hard to keep from getting up and examining the box. She would certainly be sure to ask Nicky. She enjoyed the popcorn and found it very comfortable as she sat on the couch with a blanket Nicky's mother had made, covering her legs. She had been thankful to come here and meet her. She was very kind, and loving as Tila would look upon her. She would see her shiny silver hair, and the touch of her skin was velvet and the wrinkles were very admirable and distinguished. She spoke with knowledge of her years. All Tila could do was think of her own mother and wonder what she was doing and how she was.

Nicky was finding his mind drifting to the events of the last few days and how much fun it had been. He reached up and felt his forehead recalling the golf ball that left the tender spot that was still present. He recalled telling his mother and how she laughed not for the fact that Tila threw the golf club but for the fact she could picture herself doing the very same thing in her position. Nicky knew she felt this way as she told him he deserved it and mentioned how she admired Tilas spunk. Nicky's face felt flush as he looked upon Tila eating popcorn and watching. Just as now he had spent many a times just watching her, His spell was broken as his mother asked if there was anything he would like before she turned in for the night. Nicky said no as did Tila, mom said don't be up to late you'll have to get going fairly early. Goodnight was exchanged and mother went to bed as Nicky sat closer to Tila to watch television and shared in the remainder of the snacks.

It was obvious that the thought of leaving was on both their minds for the silence was prominent in the room. That mixed with being tired was playing its toll upon Nicky and Tila. Tila told Nicky she was going to bed and kissed Nicky on the cheek. I've had so much fun, she said but I am looking forward to going back home. I've been missing Tioga and my friends and I can't wait to tell Tioga of all the things I've seen and done. I'm glad you've enjoyed yourself for I have also. Sweet dreams he said as Tila turned herself in Nicky soon was gazing out the window as his thoughts wondered about the days to come. Tila would be going home and Nicky would be going back to work. They would be apart all of the sudden the thought of her absence left an empty feeling deep inside him

It was not what he expected to feel yet at the same time it wasn't all that surprising. How could he begin to deal with the choices that would have to be made eventually Tila had become a very important part of his life? she had filled everything that was left empty in him since his fiance had been lost at sea. She had been all he had come to love and want in a woman. Yet she was more although he would catch himself thinking of his fiancee to a point of comparison he would catch himself knowing it was not fair. For there was no comparison, they both were perfect in every way. (Their own way) and the love was the same completely! Was that what he said to himself? He could not deny it, he loved Tila.

So what choices were there? She was from a different world than his as he was from hers. Their families were on one side or the other of these worlds. How could they live in two worlds? What if it came down to a choice what then? Could he possibly give up his world? What of his mother Nicky became sad, and confused once again his world was perfect and content would it end in disaster as before? Would he find himself all alone? Being alone would not be bad if it kept from hurting Tila. He would be content living in both worlds maybe!

It was all becoming too confusing. Nicky began watching television just to occupy his mind. As the hour grew late he was soon fast asleep on the couch. Nicky was tossing and turning on the couch as his mind was searching for Tila. She seemed to be across a river he could not find a way to cross. He would call to her and she would wave, not feeling the concern he was having. Yet he frantically searched for a way to reach her. Tila! Tila over here Nicky! Wake up! Nicky! Nicky woke as Tila sat on the couch near him with her hand on his shoulder. Are you okay he asked I am fine! Are you? You were calling for me in your sleep. I must have been dreaming.

Oh Tila Nicky said as he pulled Tila towards him I love you Tila! Nicky said I love you too Tila said as they kissed and embraced one another. They fell asleep on the couch with Tila laying on Nicky's shoulder. It seemed like a very short time before mother was waking them up to prepare for their journey home. What was this journey really? Was it really just a journey home or was it a journey to face reality, was it a journey of faith of love or togetherness of choosing to be apart where do they go from here feelings were shared but how far could this bonding go! After all she was a fairy from a world unlike Nicky's. Would they be able to accept not being together? There were still so many things to share and experience, but from what realm, there were sacrifices on both sides.

Nicky found himself being caught up in question after question as Tila was not so involved as he was of his concerns. At least that he could tell. It seemed as though Tila was more excited to be home and see her family and friends. Nicky decided to not push his concerns but take it day by day and deal with one hurdle at a time. As he tried to clear his mind he prepared for the train ride home. As they entered the train station Nicky and Tila pondered the future in silence. Nicodemus did not know what the future would hold for the two of them, but Nicky knew his emptiness was no longer there.

Life is an adventure who could have ever imagine having such a great friend as Tila who could ever imagine two lives so different finding one another. Nicodemus could not wait to see what the future holds for he and Tila the train pulled forward and they were on their way.

THANKS TO THE FEW WHO KNEW AND THE ONES THAT BELIEVED A VERY SPECIAL THANK YOU TO MY CHILDREN WHOM I LOVE VERY MUCH AND FOR BEING MY STORY!!!!!!!! LOVE TO MY FAMILY AND THE HELP PROVIDED BY THEM AND SUPPORT.

Printed in the United States
by Baker & Taylor Publisher Services